THE AMAZING EDIE ECKHART

ROSIE JONES

ILLUSTRATED BY NATALIE SMILLIE

HODDER

HODDER CHILDREN'S BOOKS

First published in Great Britain in 2021 by Hodder & Stoughton

1 3 5 7 9 10 8 6 4 2

A CIP catalogue record for this book
is available from the British Library.

ISBN 978 1 444 95834 8
Signed Edition ISBN 978 1 444 96571 1

Typeset in Duper by Avon DataSet Ltd, Arden Road, Alcester, Warwickshire

Printed and bound in Great Britain by Clays Ltd, Elcograf S.p.A.

The paper and board used in this book
are made from wood from responsible sources.

MIX
Paper from
responsible sources
FSC® C104740

Hodder Children's Books
An imprint of
Hachette Children's Group
Part of Hodder & Stoughton Limited
Carmelite House
50 Victoria Embankment
London EC4Y 0DZ

An Hachette UK Company
www.hachette.co.uk

This book is dedicated to you. Yes, you!

Check you out, having a book dedicated to you.

What a fancy pants.

27th August — Friday 1.33pm (AKA LUNCHTIME!)

Right now I feel like one of those really pretty women in a cute American romcom, who sits on a deck chair in a floppy hat and writes in her diary, whilst occasionally staring out to sea, as if the horizon holds all the answers to the questions she has in life. They always look *so cool*, don't they?

Unfortunately, I don't think the horizon contains the answer to the main question on my mind at the moment: when on earth are we going to go to the chip shop? A girl can only wait so long for cheesy chips and gravy! If you've never tried cheesy chips and gravy, try it! It's majorly *delicious*, honestly!

To try and distract myself from my rumbling tummy, I'm writing in my new diary. Yep, Mum thinks it's a good idea for me to write one, so here we are. Between you and me, I'm only doing it to keep her quiet.

I don't know why she's insisting on me writing a diary, because I write all the time anyway.

I write proper stuff. Poems, short stories and scripts for the telly. One day I'm gonna be the biggest writer on the planet – probably bigger than Shakespeare! Romeo and *Who*liet? Ohhhh no, people will say the greatest love story ever written is 'Snogging Scott Monroe' by Edie Eckhart. Honestly, watch this space!

Also, Mum says that if I write in my diary every day, she'll up my pocket money by a pound and you know what that means? More sausage rolls in my mouth, yes please. I love sausage rolls, and Scotch eggs, and pork pies, and . . . oh no, I'm talking about food again!! This is no good; I'm just making myself even hungrier!

Anyway, let me tell you a bit more about myself. Hello, bonjour, guten Tag! My name is Edie Eckhart. My middle name is Annie, after my mum's favourite singer, Annie Lennox, but I can't sing at all. When I sing, my dad says that it sounds like the 'cats' chorus'. Rude!

Edie

2

I am eleven years old (twelve in December, in a hundred and eight days. Not that I'm counting!) and I'm having the Best Summer Ever.

I see Oscar *every* day. He's been my best friend since reception class and he is the BEST. We've been inseparable since forever. This summer we've been watching loads of old *Carry On* films with Oscar's mum, Elaine, and pretending not to understand the rude bits. We definitely do understand. They're talking about BOOBS.

Oscar

We also eat sausage rolls whenever we can, and sometimes Maccy D's when we're feeling fancy. Oscar loves food as much as I do! And we're both starting secondary school together in September. BIG TIMES AHEAD!

Here's a few things I love, and a few things I absolutely HATE:

THINGS I LOVE

- Comic books
- Writing stories
- Dungaree dresses
- Colourful tights
- ALL FOOD (apart from anchovies)
- Jigsaw puzzles
- Funny films
- Camping
- Watching the rain (when I'm inside)
- Sweet AND salty popcorn together

THINGS I HATE

- Being proved wrong
- Cotton wool (It feels WEIRD)
- ALL MATHS
- Snow (I look like Bambi on the ice!)
- Anchovies
- Lip gloss (too sticky)
- Needles
- Arguing with Oscar
- Being outside when it's raining
- ALL SPORT (especially football!)

What else? Oh, yeah, I'm a little bit different. I have a disability called cerebral palsy. That just means brain damage. I talk slowly and I fall over a lot. Whenever I'm tired or sad I also dribble a bit. It's never really bothered me, because I've always been like this, and I've never known any different.

4

I live in a town called Bridlington, or Brid for short, in Yorkshire. It's only an eight-minute walk from my house to the beach (probably a five-minute walk for other people, but I like to factor in the wobbles!).

Let's face it, when you live near the beach, you hardly ever go, because you take it for granted.

Like, right now I'm already bored! Me and Oscar made a MEGA sandcastle, with a fort and everything, and knocked it down just for the lols, then we played catch with the beach ball, but a dog ran over and popped it with her little dachshund claws, then pooped all over our demolished sandcastle, it was so funny! The dog's owner ran over and apologised, but we told her we didn't mind. The owner said the dog was called Dolly. I wish I'd asked if she was named after Dolly Parton, I bet you a million quid she was!

I love dogs so much, and Dolly was a super, super cute dog. Me and Oscar have already decided that when we're adults and live in London in a fancy-pants town house, we're gonna get our own dog. The only problem is that Oscar wants a Chihuahua, and I want a husky (I love their bright blue eyes and how majorly cuddly they look!).

Seeing Dolly today started up the disagreement again, because Oscar said small dogs are cuter, and I think he could not be more wrong. We went back and forth on the argument, until Oscar's older sister Charlie butted in.

'You could get a cross-breed of a Chihuahua and a husky. What would you call it? A Chusky?'

Charlie laughed. 'Imagine what that would look like!' Then she said, all serious, 'So, will you get a dog before or *after* you lovebirds get married?'

Then she made loads of gross kissing noises and pretended to snog her arm. She's so annoying. Just because she's fourteen she thinks she knows everything. Mate, it's 2021. Newsflash: a boy and a girl can be friends without ending up married. Friends can share a Chusky, and eat cheesy nachos together every night, without them necessarily wanting to marry each other!

Charlie

But Charlie isn't my sister, so I just pretended not to hear her whilst Oscar gave her a dead arm. Then Oscar's dad, Ted, told him off. In Oscar's defence, she deserved it.

Charlie's full name is Charlotte, but literally nobody calls her that, apart from their great-grandma. She always has a different hairstyle, and like Oscar, she wears glasses. Today she's got her hair in two puff balls on her head, which looks amazing. She might look cool, but she is a right know-it-all sometimes, and know-it-alls can be really annoying.

YES! Oscar's mum, Elaine, just asked us if we fancy anything from the chippy. At long last, I was gonna pass out! We sure do, ma'am! Cheesy chips, gravy and mushy peas, I'm coming for ya!

7

Sunday 10.58am

It's Oscar's birthday today; he's only just turned eleven, I know, *what* a baby! I tease him about it all the time, and when I do, his eyebrows get so tight they look like two angry slugs over his glasses. He's a little bit shorter than me too, and he gets *really* angry when I bring that up!

Even though this birthday isn't any different to other birthdays we've had, it feels extra special. I think it's because we're both starting secondary school in a few days. This is the last proper birthday without any adult worries like, *where did I leave my tax form thing?* Or, *oh no, I've run out of milk!* Or, you know, other rubbish adults think about.

Anyway, every year, for two whole birthdays – mine and Oscar's – we do the same thing. It's three simple birthday steps to complete happiness, otherwise called the THREE M'S:

NUMBER ONE: We get to **McDonald's** at precisely 10:58am. We order hash browns from the breakfast menu. This is kind of like our starter. Then, GET IN, at 11am, the lunch menu becomes available. A Quarter Pounder meal each, vanilla milkshakes and six chicken nuggets to share. BOOM. The birthday meal of champions. Smashing. The. Day!

This is where I'm currently writing this diary entry – on a greasy table at Maccy D's. Here comes Oscar, back from the counter, almost falling over because he's carrying so much. What a legend! He's holding five cartons of hash browns and those little paper cups filled with delicious sugary sauce. Holy macaroni, I'm excited!

'Oi, Edie! It's my birthday, stop writing or else I'll *accidentally* spill ketchup on your new diary. You've got to hang out with me!'

Well, he is the birthday boy so I'd better do what he says. Any other day I'd just tell him to bog off! Also I can't get my paper all messy, I'm starting to feel quite attached to my diary. Don't tell Mum!

Sunday 7.02pm

I'm back home now, so I can legit write in my diary without Oscar telling me to put it away. Where was I? Oh yes, the three birthday steps! So, the rest of the THREE M'S went like this . . .

NUMBER TWO: With our bellies full of hash browns, burgers and chippies, we went back to Oscar's house and spent the day watching Marvel films, under a blanket on the sofa. Because it's Oscar's birthday, he got to pick the films. This year, he chose *Black Panther*, *Guardians of the Galaxy* and our favourite film, *Marvel Avengers Assemble*. Honestly, even if I watched that film a million times, I'd never get bored of it. Every time I watch it I see something new in it that I've never seen before.

NUMBER THREE: Elaine, Ted and Charlie joined us to play Monopoly. I'm always the iron (it's the best one) and Oscar's always the racing car. We ended up playing for ages, whilst eating salt and vinegar Chipsticks. Delightful. I don't want to blow my own trumpet, but I did win. Charlie went off in a huff, which we all thought was really hilarious. She is majorly competitive!

I think Oscar had a good day, and he really loved the presents I gave him: a Hawkeye bobble-head (Hawkeye is his favourite character), and a Marvel pencil case. I'm a bit jealous of the pencil case actually; I might nab it from him when we start at our new school next week!

Tuesday 3.43pm

I had a day off from writing yesterday because, let's face it, not every day is interesting. It wasn't bad, but not a lot happened. It's what my mum would call 'a nothing day'. My mum is so obsessed with being busy that when she doesn't have any plans, she will lits put, 'Nothing Day' on her calendar and then cross it off, because she's done nothing. Honestly, it makes no sense to me!

Anyway, I saw Oscar, we watched *Carry On Camping*, we played Kerplunk and, no surprises here, Charlie was being *super* annoying. Same. Old. Story. I think I've decided I'm only going to write entries on the days when something interesting is going on.

Today I've come shopping with Mum and my four-year-old brother Louie. We're currently sitting outside the changing room, waiting for Mum to try on the TWELFTH blouse of the day, rolls eyes. I thought we were supposed to be getting my uniform, and Louie's new primary school uniform, but Mum keeps seeing 'must-haves' for herself. Typical!

I look down at Louie. The sweatshirt he'd tried on

earlier looked massive on him. He looks much too young to be going to school; he's still my baby bro! I remember when he was born, I was so, so, so happy to have a brother, and somebody to look after. We've always been super close, even though he's seven years younger than me. We're a lot closer than Oscar and Charlie, and we don't argue half as much as they do!

Louie

'Didi?' Lou says. Lou's called me Didi since he started talking (it was his first word, which made me very happy!).

'Yes, Lou?'

'Is school scary, Didi?'

I take his little hand in mine. 'Of course it isn't, Lou-Lou, it's great!' Secretly, though, I'm a bit worried. I really want Lou to enjoy school as much as me. And I hope he finds a best friend just as brilliant as Oscar.

Me and Oscar became best friends on the first day in Reception class when he walked straight up to me and asked me what was wrong with my legs.

I told him nothing was wrong with them, and that I had cerebral palsy . . . although at the time I think I called it 'terrible palsy'. I didn't know what it meant to be disabled!

Oscar was silent for about five seconds. 'Okay,' he said. 'Do you want to play Lego?' We've been best friends ever since!

Right, better go, Mum's *finally* come out of the changing room, and, surprise surprise, she's not buying any of the blouses, not one!

5.12pm

On the way home from shopping, Mum keeps asking me if I'm nervous about starting secondary school tomorrow, but I'm not.

'It's okay to be nervous, mushroom. On my first day of secondary school, I cried so hard, your nan had to bribe me with money to stop me!'

I like it when Mum talks about her mum. She died before I was born, and my mum misses her loads, obviously. Her dad is still alive though, Grandad Eric. And if Nan was half as great as Grandad Eric, she must've been legit incredible. I wish I could've met her.

Anyway, clearly my mum's more nervous about me starting school than I am. I think it'll be great. Another adventure: me and Oscar, best friends, the dream team, partners in crime against the world, like it's always been. Bring. It. On.

Mum

15

Wednesday, 1st September – AKA the First Day of Secondary School! 5.30pm

TODAY WAS THE WORST DAY OF MY LIFE. Terrible.

I should've known it was going to be a bad day, because it was awful from the beginning.

First of all, I fell over on the way to school. Just outside the school gates, to be exact. It isn't unusual for me to fall over – on average I take a tumble about once a week, and I usually just spring back up. You know, like that Chumbawamba song.

But this was a bad fall. I'd ripped my tights, and when I looked down, my left knee was full of blood and dirt. I full-on cried, which was mega embarrassing, because people kept walking past and staring at me. It didn't hurt that much, but I didn't want to be known as 'Bloody Knee Girl' on my first day at school either. My name is Edie Eckhart and I'm proud of it, thank you very much!

Luckily, Oscar always carries an 'Edie First Aid Box' in his bag, and he patched it up with a Marvel plaster.

'Mate, shall I kiss it better?' he asked.

I kicked him away with my un-plastered leg. 'Ew, gross, absolutely not, you weirdo!'

He gave me the spare pair of tights he always carries with him in the Edie First Aid Box. He's thought of everything! The uniform code stated 'black tights' but now I was going to be noticed wearing the coolest tights known to man or woman, or alien: my fox tights. They've got lots of cute fox faces all over them, and they're my favourite things I own. I mean, if I ever ripped *those* tights I think I would probably have a full-on meltdown, no jokes.

Oscar leant down and offered me his arm. 'Edie, do you like chicken?' I nodded and grinned. 'Then take a wing.' We linked arms as we headed up the drive and into the school hall together.

☆☆☆

The school IS huge, and the hall is a lot bigger than our old school hall. Everybody is MASSIVE, like, properly tall, and all the big people were looking at us like they knew it was our first day. I could tell Oscar was nervous too, because he kept rearranging his bobble hat. But he was pretending not to be nervous, so I didn't mention it.

A woman greeted us from the reception desk. She had huge round glasses resting on her nose, and wild, blonde hair that, if I was being rude, looked like it hadn't been brushed in years. If she was my mum, I'd buy her a big hairbrush for Christmas!

'Names.'

Oi, lady, ever heard the word, 'please'? I wanted to say. But I knew that wouldn't go down well, so I kept my mouth shut.

'Oscar Jenkins, and this is Edie Eckhart,' Oscar said. It was quicker if he told the woman both of our names. He squeezed my shoulder as he did so.

The woman scrolled on her iPad. 'Oscar Jenkins, right, you're in 7MM, far right corner, and, let me see here, Edie Eckhart, you are in 7KA which is, ah, near the stage over there.' She glanced at Oscar. 'Does she need help?'

I hate people asking Oscar questions when they could ask me. Just because I wobble a bit doesn't mean I'm stupid. I get a lot of people patronising me, especially adults, and it's really annoying and stupid and BORING.

But now was not the right time to get annoyed about that. The more important thing was that ME AND OSCAR HAD BEEN PUT IN DIFFERENT CLASSES. I couldn't believe it. Like, honestly, how could they even think about splitting us up?

Oscar gave me a pep talk. 'It will be okay, I'll meet you at lunch. I'll keep hold of the first aid kit, so if you fall, we can be reunited,' he said, with a wink.

I rolled my eyes. 'I'm not a baby, Oscar, jeez. I think I'll be okay.'

We hugged before walking in opposite directions, which was obviously not the cool thing to do, because all the tall people stared at us and I suddenly felt my face go red.

When I eventually found my tutor group and sat down, most of my classmates looked at me funny. They couldn't have met anybody with cerebral palsy before. I don't think they meant to be rude. I understand they must have questions, but I wish they'd just ask, rather than staying quiet and staring at me. They think it's rude to ask. It's not. Asking means that they can get answers.

They're happy, I'm happy, and we can just all get on with our lives . . . simple!

The only good thing that happened was meeting my tutor, Mrs Adler. She's lovely, and she's really, really pregnant (she's having twins). She is *beautiful* and has long, red, curly hair, and the biggest smile in the world. She looks a bit like Grace from *Will and Grace*, which is my mum's favourite sitcom. Wait, that's funny; Grace's surname is Adler too!

☆☆☆

I got to see Oscar at lunch (we both had shepherd's pie). I told him about Mrs Adler and how nice she is, and the big news, that she's going to have baby twins soon.

'I think she might be the loveliest woman on the planet, Osc, I really do.'

'That's cool,' Oscar said, shovelling peas into his mouth. Some flew out of his mouth when he talked. 'My tutor is called Mr Murphy and he's grumpy. Grumpty Dumpty. Apparently his "hobby" is collecting tin foil and making sculptures out of it. Bit weird, innit?'

20

'I guess so. I wonder what Mrs Adler's hobby is. I bet it's something really kind, like volunteering in a dog shelter on her weekends. She's really nice.'

Oscar put his fork down. 'Will you stop banging on about Mrs Adler, when I've got to deal with the Tin Man?' He got up and started doing a robot dance.

We both fell about laughing.

'Go on, I dare you to ask him where the scarecrow is tomorrow!'

Oscar laughed harder.

'Stop it, I'm going to wee myself! Edie, mate, I miss you so much!' Oscar said, putting his arm around me. 'I miss sitting behind you and secretly playing hangman. Even though I always lost!'

I smiled. 'Well, I can't help knowing *all* the words! I might be wobbly, but I am EXTREMELY intelligent!'

Oscar pushed my arm playfully. 'Big head!'

After lunch, I didn't really speak to anybody in my class. I didn't see the point. Why bother making friends when I have Oscar, the ULTIMATE best friend?

I talked to Mum, and Oscar talked to Elaine last night and we convinced them to go and talk to the head tomorrow morning. They need to ask if we can be in the same class. We suggested Oscar join me in Mrs Adler's class, because she's clearly better than the tin foil obsessive.

They have to make it happen. Otherwise, who will give me plasters when I fall over? I *need* Oscar in my class. He's the fish to my chips, the sausage to my mash, and the bananas to my custard!

I already cried when I ripped my tights earlier, but I think I'm going to have one more giant cry before bed. Tomorrow will be better though – won't it?

AMY JOHNSON ACADEMY

Name: Edie Eckhart

Form: 7KA

Tutor: Mrs Adler

	PERIOD 1	PERIOD 2	MORNING BREAK	PERIOD 3	PERIOD 4	LUNCH BREAK	PERIOD 5	PERIOD 6
MONDAY	HISTORY *BIG fan*	ENGLISH		MATHS *Boo!*	DRAMA *YAY*		GEOGRAPHY	RELIGIOUS STUDIES
TUESDAY	SCIENCE *Boring*	COMPUTING		FRENCH *J'adore le français!*	ENGLISH		MUSIC	P.E *Would prefer to sit down for an hour*
WEDNESDAY	CITIZENSHIP	MUSIC *FUN*		SCIENCE	ART		ENGLISH	MATHS
THURSDAY	ENGLISH	MATHS		P.E	SCIENCE		D & T	FRENCH
FRIDAY	GEOGRAPHY *Who cares about rocks?*	MATHS		ENGLISH	HISTORY		SCIENCE	ART *Messy... but GREAT*

Thursday 4.12pm

Today was NOT better than yesterday. Holy moly, if anything, it was even WORSE.

I couldn't even find Oscar at lunchtime because the school is inhumanely big. BRAINWAVE! They should put a map at the front of everyone's planners. In fact, I'm going to suggest that to Mrs Adler. I bet she'll really like that idea.

Not only that, but I had P.E. today. I <u>hate</u> P.E., and not just because of my disability, I just don't see what the point of it is! Where's the fun in running around a field for no actual reason? No, thank you. Not for me. I'd rather stay inside, in a nice comfy chair, writing.

And then I was so tired after the running, I accidentally fell asleep in my science lesson.

Everybody laughed at me and it was super embarrassing.

I wish I could put the whole day in the bin. And now I'm back home, Mum is dishing up my favourite tea, lasagne, which means something is definitely up. She's about to soften a big blow. I can feel it.

Yep, here it is . . .

'Edie, love, I met with the head teacher today, and she doesn't think it would be wise for you and Oscar to be in the same tutor group. And unfortunately I have to agree with her.'

What? I can't believe what I'm hearing right now. How can my own mother side with somebody she met for lits ten minutes over her own daughter?

'I'm sorry, mushroom,' Mum sighed, pouring me and Louie a glass of water. 'You and Oscar probably have always relied on each other a bit too much up until now. Maybe this is an opportunity to make new friends.'

What is this obsession with me making new friends?! Mum is usually on the money about things but now she has veered off into minus funds forever. What is she even on about?

'I have a new friend!' Lou beamed. 'His name is Ralph!'

He looked so pleased, and started to tell us all about Ralph, who loves Lego *almost* as much as Lou does, and his favourite colour is yellow. It gave me and Mum time to calm down and not get properly shouty with each other.

I'm pleased Lou has made a friend, I almost forgot all about how bad this day was. But not quite, no. This day was an actual BIN and it can bog off.

Friday 1.03pm

IT'S ALMOST THE WEEKEND!!! Thank banana for that. It has been the slowest school week *ever*, and it was only three days long. Can't we be done with school now? I'm eleven . . . I know enough now to get by in life, don't I?

You know what, I wish I was Victorian, so I could be sent to work in a factory. That sounds much better than the fresh hell I'm going to be living for the next five years. FIVE. YEARS. That'll be nearly a third of my life! I'm going to have to transport myself back to the Victorian times. I'll start by reading one of Mum's supermarket Victorian romance novels and then I just need to hope for a small miracle. Anybody in Bridlington got a little time machine going for sale?

When I saw Oscar at lunch, we had a chat about how legit rubbish it was that we hadn't moved into each other's tutor groups. To make each other feel better, we each swapped one half of our sandwich. Mum had made me cheese (and pickle, obvs), and Elaine made Oscar jam – it sounds gross, but I dare you to eat a cheese sandwich and then a jam sandwich yourself, before you judge us. Cheese, pickle and jam is actually nice, honestly!

In between mouthfuls, I told Oscar my Victorian factory girl plan.

'Edie, mate,' he said. 'Even if you did transport yourself back in time, I don't think you'd be that useful in a Victorian factory. You'd probably trip over a cotton reel and get your head decapitated by a loom!'

I laughed so much that jam dribbled out of my mouth. Oscar passed me a tissue.

At that moment, five beautiful girls all linking arms in a row walked past. One of the girls had crazy long blonde hair, we're talking Rapunzel length.

'Hi Oscar!' she said, smiling as she walked past our table.

'Oh, hi!' Oscar mumbled through a mouthful of cheese and pickle. He grinned, and a bit of pickle sneaked out of the gap in his front teeth.

I handed him the tissue he'd just given me and nodded towards his mouth. 'I think you need this more than I do!'

Oscar turned BRIGHT RED like a tomato and the girl giggled, 'See you in class.' Then she smiled at me and waved.

'Bye!' I said, waving back.

I turned to Oscar, but I couldn't see him because he had pulled his bobble hat down over his face.

Whoever that girl was, I'm sure he fancies her.

'That girl seems nice,' I said, trying not to laugh at how obviously embarrassed Oscar was.

'Yeah that's Georgia,' Oscar said, muffled by his hat.

He always hides when he's about to tell me a secret, or something he doesn't want to admit. 'I *really* like her. She's in my tutor group with Mr Murphy. She's kind and beautiful, like, did you *see* her hair? It's like, magical or something. I think . . . I don't know, but I reckon I'd like her to be my girlfriend. What do you think?'

I couldn't believe my ears to be honest. Oscar's never had a girlfriend, and I've never had a boyfriend. We talk about fancying people, but mostly characters from comic books and TV shows, and when we talk about dating and marriage and stuff, it's usually way, way, WAY into the future. Oscar's going to marry the Black Widow and I'm going to marry Hawkeye. Then the four of us will live in the same house together with our Chusky. When our partners are away saving the world, we will hang out and play *Mario Kart* and order takeaways. We're going to be living the dream!

I smiled and lifted Oscar's bobble hat up a bit, so I could see more of his face. 'Sounds good, Osc. If you like her, I like her! Whatever makes you happy.'

Holy moly, am I clever! I've just got off FaceTime with Oscar and I've come up with a F*O*O*L*P*R*O*O*F plan to convince Mrs Adler to move him into our class. We're going to use the Card (I'll explain the Card in a minute).

On the phone Oscar also said we've been invited to Georgia's birthday party this weekend. WINNING! Maybe I will make new friends after all. Oscar says he wants me to be his wingman for a change. I don't really get what that means; is it something to do with chicken wings? But I agreed anyway.

So the Card is something that we invented when we discovered that adults (especially teachers) will believe ANYTHING, as long as I blame it on my disability. I know it's cheeky, but why shouldn't I use my 'disadvantage' to my advantage?

I've used the Card loads to get out of small stuff. The first time was back in Year 4, when me and Oscar were so engrossed in a comic (*Spider-Man: Life Story*), we didn't hear the bell ring for the end of lunch. When we looked up, absolutely nobody was left in the playground apart from us.

It felt like the quiet aftermath of an Armageddon scene in a Marvel film. I was half-expecting Thanos to appear from behind the school. It would have been quite cool, only we both HATE getting told off. Oscar goes bright red and attempts to hide under his hat (classic Oscar), and my lip wobbles as much as my legs.

'RATS ON TOAST!' we both said, panicking and getting up from the bench.

'What are we going to do?' said Oscar.

'We could just say I fell over and you were helping me,' I said.

Oscar shook his head. 'That won't work. You know I'm a terrible liar, Edie.'

'We don't have a choice. How else are we going to explain why we're late? Don't worry, you can just stand behind me and keep quiet.'

Oscar grabbed my arm and off we wombled to class. On our way, we picked up a few twigs and leaves and styled them in my hair for extra va-va-voom. I had to be sure that our teacher would fall for it.

When we opened the door, Mr Sheldon was there. He was a cuddly, grandad sort of a man who always wore cardigans, but had a surprising mean streak. He shot us a deadly look and furrowed his eyebrows.

'Edie and Oscar, you're extremely late! Where have you been?'

The whole class turned to stare. Oscar's arm tensed under mine. I gulped. Would Mr Sheldon see through me? Maybe, but there was only one way to find out.

'Sorry sir, I – I fell over.' I retrieved a leaf from my hair, and held it up like a trophy, as if it proved I was telling the truth.

Mr Sheldon's face changed, like someone had smoothed out his eyebrows. 'Oh Edie, are you okay? Do you want to visit the nurse to get checked out?'

I shook my head bravely. 'I think I'll be okay, sir.'

PHEW! HE BELIEVED US! Honestly, my performance deserved a BAFTA. Piece of cake. It took everything I had not to high-five Oscar right then and there.

After that, Oscar kept going on about me becoming an actor one day. I think I'd be better off writing plays, myself.

Since then, we've used the Card when we couldn't be bothered to queue for cake at Greggs, or wanted more time to hang out together, or just fancied being as flaky as the flakiest sausage rolls once in a while. It's the superpower that keeps on giving . . . and it's all ours!

So our plan is to use the Card on Mrs Adler. If I say that Oscar and I have to be in the same class because I need him to help me, then she'll have no choice but to move him.

Easy peasy lemon squeezy.

Wednesday 1.13pm

I *HATE* MRS ADLER!!!!!! I take back everything I said about her being the loveliest woman on the planet. She's the worst woman in the WORLD. In fact, she's probably not even a human being . . . she must be made of STONE.

Oscar puts his hand gently on my shoulder. 'Careful Edie, if you scribble that hard in your diary, you might tear the page! Calm down!'

News flash: telling somebody to 'calm down' never helps. If anything, it makes somebody even *more* annoyed! I can't believe Oscar isn't as angry as I am.

Here's what happened.

After registration this morning I waited until everybody had left and asked Mrs Adler if I could talk to her about something that had been 'worrying me'.

'Mrs Adler, Oscar is the only person at school who understands me and what I need,' I said, opening my eyes very wide, and wobbling my bottom lip as if I were about to cry. 'For example, do you know that Oscar carries a first aid box just for me, because I fall over a lot?

35

He carries an extra pair of tights, in case I rip mine. I really need him to be with me at all times.'

BAFTA worthy performance! A 10/10 delivery, I thought.

Mrs Adler sighed. 'You have a bag, Edie. Why not carry your own pair of tights?'

What was that supposed to mean? This wasn't going how I expected.

Mrs Adler leant back against her desk. 'Secondary school is different, Edie. I'm not going to sugar-coat it for you. There will be times, now, and later in life, which will be especially hard for you.'

I stared at her. She was smiling faintly. I couldn't work out whether she was being patronising or not.

'I've only known you for a week,' she went on, 'but I can already see that you are strong and independent. You do not need Oscar, or anybody else, to carry tights for you. Use this new start, and my utmost confidence in you, to realise how brilliantly able you are on your own.'

Brilliantly able? I'm *literally* the opposite. I am DIS-abled. Clearly Mrs Adler was talking out of her bum, and has never met anybody like me before.

My lip wobbled and I walked out of her classroom before I full-on bawled like a baby in front of her. The Card had never failed before, and now I didn't know what to do.

☆☆☆

'Come on, Edie. Let's play hangman! It will cheer us up,' Oscar says now. He is right. He always is.

We're sat on our favourite bench, in the quad. We've both wolfed down our sandwiches in record time, so now it's hangman time!

While I think of my hangman phrase, Oscar adjusts his bobble hat over his fringe. 'Oh, also, Edie, I reckon I'm going to join the football club.'

Umm, this news is even weirder than Oscar fancying that Georgia girl. I've known him for seven years and he's never mentioned football once. I don't know what to say, so I don't say anything. My silence says it all.

'I just want to try out new things and make a few new friends. Don't worry though, you'll always be my best friend!'

I suddenly feel a bit sick, but I smile through it.

I playfully bash Oscar on the arm.

'Yeah, but football? I'm the dribbler, not *you*!'

Oscar snorts with laughter and puts his arm around me. 'I love you, Edie!'

Wednesday 6.20pm

Later that evening, Mum's in the kitchen arranging custard creams on a plate. She's half-distracted, so now will be a good time to ask my question.

'Mum, can I go to Georgia's birthday party on Saturday?'

'Who is Georgia, and is Oscar going?'

'She's a girl in my year, and yes, Oscar is going. He knows her better than I do, and apparently she's really nice.'

'Okay, great, sure, mushroom.' She turns around and smiles. 'It'll be a good opportunity to make new friends.'

Still with the obsession about me making new friends. That's what she said when she wouldn't stick up for me when I wanted to move tutor groups to be with Oscar! I don't need new friends. I have Oscar.

Grandad Eric walks into the kitchen when we're talking about the party. He has come round for tea, like he normally does on a Wednesday. Dad has an evening shift, so won't be home until the early morning, which sucks.

Dad's a doctor, a paediatrician to be exact, which means that he takes care of children and some of them are disabled. It's funny that a man who takes care of disabled children happens to have a kid who is disabled, but he said it was meant to be. What better person to bring up a disabled baby than somebody whose job it is to take care of disabled babies!

He loves his job, and Mum jokes that he's a workaholic, and even though I'm happy that he's out there saving children and babies it doesn't stop me missing him loads. He's a good man.

But when Dad is at work, I see my Grandad Eric loads. He is basically my second dad, and he is a proper legend! Sometimes he even takes me and picks me up from school, when I'm not walking with Oscar, that is.

Mum offers Grandad Eric a custard cream. He takes one and beams.

'Thanks, Angela, love.' Then he looks at me. 'Don't go mad at this party, Edie. And if anyone gives you any trouble, they'll have my fist to deal with!' Grandad Eric crumbles a biscuit in his hand to make his point.

I laugh. He worries a lot about me, more than anybody I know, and a lot of people think he's grumpy and miserable. Even Dad is a bit scared of him! But I'm not. I know, deep down, he's a big softie.

Now Grandad Eric is launching into one of his classic topics of conversation. Recently some teenagers have been hanging out at the front of Grandad Eric's house. 'The toerags have been on my front lawn again, with their beer cans and their dirty cigarettes. But don't you worry. I chased them right away with my broom.'

'You can't keep doing that, Dad!' Mum sighs. 'It's dangerous, you don't know what those kids will do!'

Grandad Eric laughs, 'I'd like to see them try!' He holds up his now-empty hands like a boxer, and winks at me. 'I was a prize fighter in my day!'

I giggle and Mum rolls her eyes. 'Oi Edie! Don't

encourage Rocky over there! He's nearly eighty and he could really injure himself!'

Grandad Eric bats the air, as if he's batting my Mum's words away. 'Oh shush, I am seventy-seven, stop trying to wish my life away!' And with that, he gets up from the chair and does a karate kick.

I laugh loudly and even Mum can't help but smile.

Grandad Eric

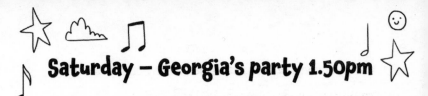

Saturday – Georgia's party 1.50pm

Everyone in Georgia's garden seems a bit nervous. I suppose we've only been at school for two weeks, so not a lot of people know each other yet, apart from the people who went to the same primary school.

Georgia's mum has cleverly set up a separate gazebo for her friends so she can stay out of our way, whilst also keeping an eye on us. So far, I've counted five prosecco corks flying out of her tent and loads of whooping and giggling.

Earlier when we were getting ready, I had an idea.

'Do you maybe want to play the Card, Oscar? We could call Georgia and say that I'm feeling tired, and just stay here at my house, eat sausage rolls and watch movies all afternoon.'

'Nah, Edie, I really think we should go, mate. It'll be fun!'

Oscar was looking at himself in the mirror, re-styling his hair, making sure it was just right.

'Why are you doing all of

that, when you're just gonna put a hat on and ruin your mop!'

He frowned, then put his hat on, proving me right.

I decided to wear my new Converse to the party. Bright red lace ups – they are so on fleek. I try to keep my new ones for best, because I hate scuffing the toes and getting them dirty, but today's party feels like a good excuse to dress up. And they match my red lobster dunga dress perfectly.

'Photo before we go?' Oscar grinned, snapping us in the mirror on his phone.

Grandad Eric drove us to the party. We ate humbugs and sang along to *ABBA Gold* in the car.

'Edie love, don't *you* be getting any man after midnight!' he said when we got to Georgia's house.

Lol. He says this every time we listen to that song.

'I won't, Grandad, don't worry!'

'And Oscar, you ladies' man, don't you be getting any girls after midnight either!'

Oscar laughed and went a bit red. 'Word. Thank you for driving us, Eric.'

'And are you sure you're okay walking back home?'

We nod enthusiastically. Secretly, I love it when we're allowed to walk home. It makes me feel proper grown-up!

Now we're here, it turns out Oscar knows some of the boys from his first football practice 😊, so he's started chatting to them. To be fair, he keeps trying to bring me into the conversation but the chat would make much more sense if I knew who some guy called Sergio Aguero was.

So instead I've come to sit on a deckchair, and I'm writing in my diary. I'm going to take a deep breath and get something to drink from the buffet table on the lawn. Writing it in here will make it happen! Go Edie! You can do this!

☆☆☆

After that, something interesting happened.

First off, I poured half the lemonade on to the grass – and I only had one sip! I hate plastic cups so much.

'Try putting one cup inside another,' came a voice from behind me. 'It makes them sturdier, and easier to drink out of.'

I turned around to see a girl looking down at the ground. 'Hi. I'm Floriana – everybody calls me Flora. Sorry for being bossy. My mum calls me Fussy McFusserson.'

Flora looked very serious, her eyebrows tight together in concentration.

I laughed, and she looked up, relieved. 'I'm excited to try the two-cup trick,' I said. 'I've lost count of the times I've squeezed a plastic cup and the drink has gone everywhere. I can't believe I've never thought of doing it before. I'm Edie, everyone calls me Edie.'

Flora poured herself a drink in a double cup too (obvs) and without saying anything she held out her arm for me to grab on to. We walked over to two beanbags in a corner of the garden and sank into them.

'Well, I'm never getting up from here now, I'm stuck!'

Flora giggled. 'Me too. So, how do you know Georgia?'

'I don't, really. I'm only here because my friend Oscar fancies her.'

Flora laughed. 'Everybody fancies Georgia! I know her because my mum is friends with her mum.'

Just then, we heard a roaring, infectious laugh from the mums' tent. 'That'll be Mum,' says Flora, cringing.

'I really like your Converse!' she said, changing the subject.

'Thanks!' I beamed, happy that she noticed my new shoes. 'Your shirt is so cool!'

To be honest, her whole outfit was majorly cool. She was wearing an old-school *Buffy* tee, skinny jeans and black shoes. It felt a bit try-hard to say,

Flora

'Hello, I like your shirt – and your jeans, and your trainers, and your hair,' so I leave it at her shirt, even though I want to compliment everything about her!

'Thanks. Have you seen *Buffy*?' she asked.

I shook my head.

'I really like it. You remind me of a character in it, Willow.'

I made a mental note to look up *Willow Buffy* when I got home, to see whether it was a compliment or not.

After that, me and Flora didn't get up from the beanbags all afternoon. Georgia's mum kept appearing to top up our drinks and hand out Party Rings. It was perfect.

Me and Flora talked about school. She's in the year above. She said she found it hard to make friends at first too, mainly because everyone thinks she's rude when they meet her.

I had to stop myself laughing when she said that, because she *is* quite serious, and it struck me then that she's probably just a bit shy. She didn't seem too shy as

the party carried on though – by the end she was talking more than I was!

She said that she wants to be an illustrator when she's older, and she showed me a few of her drawings on her phone.

'They're just silly little doodles.'

They were more than that. The illustrations were so detailed, and bright. It must've taken her HOURS to draw them. 'Flora, these are Brilliant with a capital B!'

She asked me loads of things about my disability, and I happily answered the usual questions:

'Will you get better?' (no)

'Will you get worse?' (no)

'Does your brother have CP too?' (no, it's not genetic)

I don't think she asked the questions to be rude though. She seemed *genuinely* interested, like she wanted to know more about me. I felt like we could've talked for days and days and days without ever stopping for breath.

Then she asked me a question I'd never ever been

asked before. 'Do you reckon you'd be different if you weren't disabled?'

I hesitated. I've always been disabled, so I've never really thought about what I could've been like if I wasn't and I was just like everybody else. I decided to think about her question seriously, so I didn't answer right away. But the silence was a good silence, not an awkward one.

I was still thinking about my answer when we were interrupted by a huge load of cheers and claps coming from the kitchen.

'They must have brought the cake out,' Flora said, and we squirmed our way out of the beanbags. Impressively, I rolled out of mine like a sneaky worm, and then got up from the ground like a pro.

We followed the noise and barged our way through a big circle of people to see . . . OSCAR and GEORGIA standing by the fridge, locking lips.

Someone started chanting, 'Oscar and Georgia sitting in the tree, K-I-S-S-I-N-G.'

Kissing? Gross! Vomaccino overload! But they were right.

Oscar beamed to the crowd, a bit of pink lip gloss sparkling on his top lip. He looked beyond happy.

☆☆☆

On our way home Oscar wouldn't stop going on about Georgia.

'Georgia said that it was her birthday wish for me to ask her out, like proper boyfriend and girlfriend, so I asked her and she said yes in front of all of her friends. And then she kissed me . . . did you see, Edie?'

'Yes I did. Everybody cheesing saw it, Osc!'

There was a spring to Oscar's step. It was quite hard to keep up to be honest; it was as if happiness was speeding him up.

'Oi! Slow down, lover boy! A girl can only wobble so fast!'

Oscar stopped and waited for me to catch him up. When I did, he grabbed my shoulders. 'I can't believe we've only been at secondary school two weeks and I've already got a girlfriend. This year is gonna be brilliant!'

I nodded and wiped his cheek, my fingers now

sparkling with Georgia's lip gloss. Oscar hugged me goodbye at my gate and then practically skipped off down the street.

He didn't give me the chance to tell him about my beanbag chat with Flora. I didn't even ask him to help me work out the answer to her brilliant big question. It's fine though; I'll ask him tomorrow, when he's less gaga on love!

Tuesday 8.48am

I don't want to become one of those grumpy teenagers who write down their worries and complaints in a notebook or a diary, but here we are. I'm not even a teenager yet so, whatever. At least I'm not listening to heavy rock yet, like Charlie.

It's been over a week since I wrote an entry because not much has really happened. It has all been totally Uneventful with a capital U.

School (without Oscar, even though he's actually there – will explain), come home, eat, bed. Repeat until the end of time. I thought I might see Flora at school but I haven't bumped into her once since the party. Maybe I made her up?

I guess it's because she's in the year above and has a different schedule. Please, oh please, dear diary, transport me to a Victorian factory. I will spin the finest cotton and I promise that I won't be decapitated by a loom . . .

Okay, to get you up to speed with things, basically: my best friend has been abducted. The old Oscar Jenkins is no more. My Oscar – the silly, old-movie-loving, sausage-roll-chicken-nugget-hash-brown-eating, red-bobble-hat-wearing goofball has been replaced by a football-loving, Georgia-kissing buffoon. I'm still the same! *Where is Oscar Jenkins? Earth to Oscar Jenkins!*

We still walk to school together, but most days Georgia walks with us. She is making a huge effort to try and be my friend, but the bottom line is that we just don't have *anything* in common.

Georgia loves:

1) Floral dresses
2) K-pop
3) Make-up

Edie loves:

1) Dungarees and Converse
2) Stevie Wonder
3) Lits every character in the Marvel universe (apart from War Machine, who is a way less cool Iron Man)

Also, although she's really friendly, she puts her foot in it all the time. Like today for instance.

On our way to school, she was like: 'I like your shoes. Do you wear those shoes because of your, erm . . .'

She meant, *do you wear those shoes because of your disability*.

'No, of course I don't! We don't have special shoes just for us!'

The really weird thing is that I was wearing my awesome red Converse and I'd still choose to wear them if I wasn't disabled, duh.

Even weirder than that – she seemed scared of the word 'disabled', as if it's a bad swear word, or maybe she thinks I don't know I'm disabled and I might burst into tears if she breaks the news.

NEWS FLASH: Edie Eckhart has a disability.

Yeah right. More like:

NEWS FLASH: Oscar Jenkins has been abducted by aliens and a girl who looks like Rapunzel and acts as if she is Rapunzel and has never been in the real world before.

I wanted to say, *you can say 'disabled', Georgia, it's not a bad word you know, it won't make me sad if you remind me that I walk and talk differently to most people. It's fine. It doesn't bother me, and you shouldn't be bothered by it either!*

But I just shook my head in disbelief.

Oscar said, 'I've got a pair of Converse too! Well, I did have, but my stupid feet grew too much this summer and now they don't fit. I still try to squeeze my feet into them every now and again, but it hurts.'

'Yeah, your feet might have grown, Oscar, mate, but you're still super short. Shame your body didn't grow with them. Am I right, Georgia?'

I don't know why I said it. I think I was trying to gang up against Oscar – girls together! But it didn't work, and Georgia looked at me like I'd said something really, really mean. Obvs it was a Joke with a capital J.

Oscar rolled his eyes at me, but still looked smug. After all, he had done what he does best: moved the conversation on without it getting weird and awkward because somebody had brought up my cerebral palsy. He's good at that – he's had years and years of practice!

When we got to school, I picked up my pace and headed off to tutor group quick-sticks, mainly because I didn't want to wait in the corridor with Romeo and Juliet smooching each other's faces off. Gross. Not for me. Bin please!

'Blimey, you're early, Edie! How's your week going?' Mrs Adler asked me, as I walked into the classroom.

She was putting up a display on the wall about collective nouns. I *almost* smiled when I read the board: *Who knew that a group of unicorns is called a BLESSING of unicorns?*

I didn't feel like telling Mrs Adler about my week when *she's* the reason it's been terrible. If she'd listened to me, and let Oscar move classes, we'd still be as close as ever. There'd be no new friends, probably no football and definitely no Georgia.

Am I a bad person because I don't want Oscar and Georgia to be boyfriend and girlfriend? I know that Georgia makes Oscar happy, but he was already happy when we used to hang out more. And I was definitely a *lot* happier.

Mrs Adler ignored the fact that I wasn't engaging in conversation and carried on. 'You know, Edie, I *hated* school when I was your age,' she said, coming over to perch on the desk in front of me. 'I just hated it. I didn't feel like I fitted in and I . . .'

Mrs Adler stopped and winced, rubbing her giant bump. Then she relaxed and laughed. 'Oh boy, Bert and Ernie are having a boxing match today!'

I snorted with laughter. I couldn't help it. 'Are you really going to call your twin babies Bert and Ernie?'

Mrs Adler smiled and shook her head. 'No, my wife and I are still very much in the workshopping baby names phase, but we love *Sesame Street*. Last week we were referring to them as Big Bird and Oscar the Grouch.'

'I know an Oscar the Grouch,' I said. 'Be careful what you wish for.' Mrs Adler winked at me.

Mrs Adler's wink made me feel like I could trust her. Maybe she wasn't so bad after all. I took a deep breath. 'Mrs Adler, you know you said the other day that life will be hard for me?'

Mrs Adler nodded. She pulled out the chair next to me and sat down.

Mrs Adler

'Well, I've been thinking about it. I wanted to know why you think that, just because I happen to talk and walk differently to most people.'

Mrs Adler quietly exhaled, looking up in thought. 'The world is full of loads of brilliant, different people, and diverse voices,' she said at last. 'But sometimes, people don't know what to do with someone, quote, "different" and that means that the person is met with confrontation, or difficulty. *Different* just means anything that isn't the norm – in terms of the colour of your skin, or your sexuality,' she pointed at herself, 'or your disability.' She pointed at me. 'Edie, when you walk in every morning, your smile lights up the room. I love your enthusiasm. Your disability might make certain things harder, and you might meet some people with old-fashioned attitudes who don't think you're as capable as everyone else, but you are. And don't forget it!'

I thought about what Mrs Adler had said. Some things might be harder for me, like walking, or rollerblading, or tying my shoelaces, but I shouldn't let that stop me from doing all the things I want to do; if anything, it makes me *more* determined to do them. Apart from rollerblading. I would be truly terrible at that and I would prefer *not* to break my face!

The bell rang. 'Oh, before class starts, I wanted to give you this,' Mrs Adler said. 'I think you would be perfect for it! Have a think about it.' She took a leaflet out of her pocket and handed it to me. Just then, everyone started filtering into the classroom, so I put the leaflet in the back of my diary to look at later.

I started chatting to Isaiah who sits next to me. He's really nice, and loves talking as much as I do, but he is *obsessed* with trains.

'What's your favourite train, Edie?' he asked me.

'Erm, I thought all trains were the same?'

'Time to stop your chattering now,' Mrs Adler said. 'We've got some nouns to learn.'

As she got going with the lesson, I remembered what she had said: 'my *wife* and I'.

Wife! Mrs Adler didn't look like a lesbian. But then again, I don't know what lesbians look like; I've never met one in real life. I just assumed that they all had short hair and looked like Clare Balding.

☆☆☆

'Did you have a good day at school, mushroom?' my mum asked me during tea. Dad was working late again so it was just the three of us.

I nodded and smiled as cheerfully as I could, considering the circumstances. I'd had to share Oscar with Georgia again at lunch today.

I chased a load of peas around my plate, like they were running away from me. We were having sausages and mash, and Louie was making a fort with his potato.

'Didi, look, it's a castle!' Louie grinned at me.

'That's nice, Lou. Now eat a few more bits of sausage, there we go!' Mum encouraged him.

At that moment, I decided to tell them about the leaflet Mrs Adler gave me this morning. 'The school is doing a Christmas play, and I think I might audition.'

Mum clapped her hands with excitement. 'Oh Edie, you'll be a star!'

I snorted. 'No, Mum! Not to act. I'm going to see if they need help *writing* the play.'

Mum nodded. 'Oh, right. What play is it?'

'*A Christmas Carol.*'

'Love, I think that's already been written!'

I rolled my eyes at her and went back to chasing peas around my plate.

She obvs didn't understand why Mrs Adler gave me the leaflet. I'm a writer, and she wanted to encourage me to do more writing. I underestimated her. Mrs A is one smart lady!

Thursday 8.04am

Okay, now it's time for me to stop feeling sorry for myself and get proactive. When Thor was stripped of his power and banished to Earth by Odin, did he mope around and throw his hammer out of the pram? No, he didn't. He got on with it, bossed around Earth and found love, like an absolute legend.

So now it's time for me to Thor it up. If Oscar has a girlfriend, I'm going to get myself a boyfriend. I've even written a list about why I should have a boyfriend and the conclusion is absolute: GET A BOYFRIEND ASAP.

REASONS TO HAVE A BOYFRIEND:

- Oscar and Georgia, me and THE BOYFRIEND will go on double dates. I won't be Gooseberry McGooseberry-Face on my own.

- THE BOYFRIEND will carry my books for me, hold

doors open for me and tell me I look pretty, every single day.

- THE BOYFRIEND will make me laugh and hold my hand when we go to the cinema.

- Lits EVERYBODY in my year has probably had a boyfriend or girlfriend already, or at least kissed someone ONCE, and I don't want to be left out.

- Kissing looks FUN.

- I'm nearly twelve – this is what happens in life. A girl goes to secondary school and gets a boyfriend. My mum and dad are always going on about how they *met* at school. So who knows – one day, THE BOYFRIEND might turn into THE HUSBAND. THE HUSBAND will make me my favourite food every single day. Pancakes for brekkie, followed by hash browns. Lunch will be jam and cheese sandwiches, and tea will be pizza with extra pepperoni. WINNING!

Potential boys to become my boyfriend:

1) Bobby. One of Oscar's new football mates. I talked to him briefly at Georgia's party. He seems really friendly and smiley.

2) Isaiah. In my tutor group. He's nice, but there would be a *lot* of train chat.

3) Henry Witty. In my science class. He's quite clever and very shy, which suits me, because I LOVE talking. He can just be quiet and listen to me, which is lits the dream relationship.

It can't be *that* hard to find a boyfriend. Oscar found a girlfriend in a week and he's a full-on ignoramus!

I told Oscar my plan in the school hall and he thinks it's a great idea. The only part he disagrees with is me asking the boy out. Oscar said that I should wait until the boy asks *me* out.

I told Oscar, 'Stop living in Roman times. It's 2021, if a girl wants to ask a boy out, she should be able to.

There's no rules, mate!'

'Okay, okay. Edie, you go for it. Conversation over.'

'Actually there is one more thing.' I suddenly felt really nervous. 'What if no boy will want to go out with me because of the Palsy?'

'Don't worry, Edie, mate – any boy at school would be lucky to go out with you, and your disability makes you superhuman cool. Anyway, if Stephen King can find a wife, we can definitely find you a boyfriend – he was waaaaay more disabled than you!'

'Stephen King? Do you mean Stephen *Hawking*?'

'Oh yeah, that's who I meant. I knew it was one of those old white guys!'

See? What an ignoramus.

'Anyway, superhuman Edie Eckhart. See you later, yeah?' Oscar said with a wink, and ran off.

Leaving me alone with my goal. Before Christmas I *will* find a boyfriend. And then, who knows? Me and THE BOYFRIEND will probably kiss under the mistletoe!

Lunchtime

Okay, so maybe getting a boyfriend is going to be a little harder than I thought it would be. Now we're older, there seems to be a lot more to being in a relationship than there was before. I mean, for starters, you need to *actually* talk to each other, and you need to truly like each other. It's a minefield! It used to be simple at primary school.

'Do you want to go out with me?'

'Yes.'

'Cool. Bye.'

And that would be it! Every so often you'd see him in the playground and you'd point to him and say to the person next to you, 'See him, there, yeah that one with the face, yeah, he's my boyfriend.'

I didn't have a boyfriend myself though, because I had Oscar. I remember the Year 6 leaving disco – all the girls were on one side of the hall and the boys were on the other, like they were properly allergic to each other. Me and Oscar were in the middle of the dancefloor, doing the robot, obvs, from the very first song to the very last! But times have changed, clearly, and eventually we must all grow up . . .

So, it's lunchtime in the quad and I am eating my sausage roll on my own, which is absolutely fine. I'm not lonely at all.

Okay, that's a lie, I *am* lonely, but more than that, I am *so angry* with Oscar! He said he would meet me here, but never showed up. And then I remembered. Yep, Oscar has football practice. GREAT! Nice one, Oscar Jenkins; thanks for nothing!

It's approximately thirteen hundred hours (1pm in normal hours) and because I have nothing better to do, I decide to approach Henry Witty and ask him to be my new boyfriend. After all, why not? He's on the bench opposite me right now, so why not? Operation Ask Henry Witty Out is go.

Henry is currently eating his sandwiches and reading a book, on his own, as usual. Perfect. I can't see what he's reading, but I'll break the ice by commenting on whatever it is. Then I'll ask him out. What a plan! Easy Peasy with a capital E and a capital P!

I'm going for it! I am going over to him, because I am a twenty-first-century girl on a mission!

Walking . . . walking . . . walking. He's looking up from his book. We have eye-contact. I repeat, we have eye-contact. I have a tight knot in my belly. What if he says no? What if he laughs at me? Just keep smiling, Edie. Almost there . . .

SPLAT. OUCH.

My chin stings. I've ripped my tights, hundo per cent. Emergency tights stash needed.

Oh, mouldy bin juice! I've tripped over NOTHING! Sometimes my legs do that and I can't explain why. It usually happens when I'm tired; it's like my legs have minds of their own and they make the decision for me. 'Nope, Edie, I know you want to walk over there, but actually, we can't be bothered today – sorry!' *Face plants the ground*.

I don't want to look up because I guarantee Henry is

laughing at me. Why am I such a banana? They always say a boy wants a girl to fall at their feet, but I don't think *this* is what they meant. I must find Oscar. He has my spare tights. But then I remember; he's at football practice.

I just need to bite the bullet, get up, look at Henry and say something funny like, 'Whoops, that was a real nice trip!'

1-2-3. Right, I'm going to look now . . .

Great. Henry is oblivious, engrossed in his book. I must have imagined the locking eyes situation before, to make it seem a bit more *Pride and Prejudice*. Maybe he's not the right boy for me; if a girl can fall at his feet and he doesn't bat an eyelid, romance IS dead.

'That doesn't look comfy!' I look up to see Flora grinning at me. She stops smiling when she sees my face and crouches down to my level.

'Edie, your chin is bleeding! Do you want to go and see the first aider?'

'Nah, no point. By now I'm a professional faller-over. Don't worry, I just wash my face and get on with it.'

'All right then.' She holds out her hand to me and

yanks me up, and we head to the nearest bathroom.

At the sinks, I wash my face. Flora rolls up her sweatshirt and reveals a massive scar on her elbow. 'I fell off my skateboard last summer and needed loads of stitches. I fall over so much, and I can't even blame it on a disability!' We laugh. She's funny, this Flora.

The bell rings, and Flora gently wipes the last bit of blood from my chin, and we head back out.

'See ya, then. I hope next time I see you it's in a much less bloody situation!' Flora says, walking up the corridor.

I wave , hoping the same thing.

New cuts: 1

Pairs of tights ripped: 1

Boys asked out: 0

Boyfriend gained: 0

Friends made: 1

I like Flora. I like her a lot.

Friday 4.27pm

'You asked out *Henry Witty*?' Oscar asks me, for the sixth time. He's been laughing ever since I told him.

I roll my eyes. I keep telling him that I never *physically* asked Henry out because before I could, I *physically* stacked it!

'Some chin gash you've got there, by the way. I'm sorry you had to clean it up on your own. You can always come and find me at footy practice if you need me, you know?'

'Thanks, Osc, but it's quite hard coming to get you when I've fallen OVER. Anyway, I didn't clean it up on my own, Flora helped me.'

Oscar furrows his thick eyebrows, making them appear from under his hat, like two slugs who have just woken up from their hibernation. He always acts like this when I mention someone new. He's allowed to have a million football friends AND a girlfriend, but when somebody helps me just once, he gets super jealous.

'Who is Flora?' Oscar asks, and he would KNOW already, if he hadn't been so wrapped up in his smooch fest at Georgia's party.

Still, I'll take my wins where I can and I am happy that I *finally* have a chance to tell Oscar all about Flora. 'She's a girl from the year above. I met her at Georgia's party when you were kissing your girlfriend. Flora's amazing actually,' I continue, looking for a rise in the eyebrow slugs, knowing exactly how to wind him up even further. 'Yeah, I think I might ask her to be my new best friend.'

Potential new best friend?

I hate arguing with Oscar, but I don't see why it should be one rule for him and another rule for me.

'*I'm* your best friend, Edie! Anyway, I know what'll cheer you up,' Oscar says excitedly. 'I've got a big football game on Thursday. You can watch with Georgia, and there might even be some boys to ask out. Properly this time.'

GREAT! I can hardly contain my excitement. NOT.

74

Sunday 9.05pm

I am actually excited for school tomorrow. Yes, you did read correctly, I am excited . . . for school!

It's audition day for *A Christmas Carol*, and I've written down *so* many suggestions for how we could make the show even better, including:

- *Why can't Scrooge be female?*
- *What if Tiny Tim dies at the end?*
- *Can Scrooge die at the end?*
- *Can Bob Cratchit die at the end?*
- *Can we set it in the future?*

I hope whoever is in charge of the play likes my suggestions! Mum is still banging on about me auditioning to *act* in the play but I keep telling her that she's got the total wrong end of the stick.

Obvs Mrs Adler didn't want me to act in the play – she knows that I want to be a writer.

Holy macaroni – this could be the start of my career as a playwright! This is *so* exciting, and I need to make sure that I make a good impression. Shakespeare, Dickens . . . Eckhart. One day, people will go and see plays written by 'the amazing Edie Eckhart'.

I go to bed, dreaming of my name in lights.

Monday 3.50pm – THE AUDITION

I head into the hall, clutching my notebook full of ideas. But when I get there – oh, wait, oh no, the Head of Drama is . . . surely not . . . Mr Murphy, Oscar's tutor! Oscar said he's always so moody, I'm already a bit scared of him.

It makes sense though; I reckon his obsession with making tin foil sculptures probably comes from performing in an am-dram play as the Tin Man in *The Wizard of Oz*, just wishing he had a heart. Wait until I tell Oscar. He'll wee himself with laughter.

'Eckhart,' yells Mr Murphy, launching himself from the stage and heading over, in a bright green jumper and a big green tie. He looks like the Incredible Hulk.

'You're nice and early, that's a good start.' My tummy turns and whirls as if somebody's just plopped it in a food blender. Why do I suddenly feel so nervous?

I take a deep breath. 'I thought, you, er, that, er, you might want a script writer, for the play,' I say, dribbling a bit from nerves.

Mr Murphy laughs. He doesn't seem like a man who

laughs often, so his whole face lights up when he does. Then he looks a bit sheepish for laughing.

'Well yes, there have been some great interpretations, but I'm a sucker for the classics. We'll be working from the original script this time. Sorry, Edie.'

Um, so rude. He sounds exactly like my mum!

He leans forward. 'Hmm, let's see here. Are these your script notes?'

I hand them over and he glances through them. '*Why can't Scrooge be female?*' he reads. 'You do have a point there. So will you be auditioning for the role of Scrooge today?'

Of *course* I'm not auditioning for the role of Scrooge. I'm not auditioning for *any* character. Me, an actor, can you even imagine? I nearly burst out laughing at the thought!

'No, sir. I'm a writer, not an actor.'

He raises his eyebrows. 'Charlie Chaplin, Orson Welles, Alan Bennett – they were all writers *and* actors! Go on, have a go. What have you got to lose?'

I have no idea who any of these people even are. All men though, from the sound of it; classic.

Mr Murphy hands me a freshly printed script from underneath his list of names, takes a chair from a stack down the side of the hall, and sits. I feel a bit sick. Is he waiting for me to do the audition right now?

'Whenever you're ready, please read the highlighted lines for Scrooge.' Mr Murphy smiles, as if it's the most normal thing in the world to just ask somebody to audition with absolutely no preparation time whatsoever.

I have an idea. The Card!

'But, Mr Murphy,' I say. 'I had no idea that Scrooge had cerebral palsy!'

He laughs again. 'Edie, if you have an acting career, not all the characters you play will necessarily be disabled.'

I don't understand. I *am* disabled; and no matter how I act, I won't ever not be disabled. Not even Meryl Streep has acting skills so good she could cure cerebral palsy!

Mr Murphy looks at his watch, a clear sign I need to get on with it. I clear my throat.

'Ghost of the Future,' I begin, gripping the script for dear life, so hard my knuckles go white, 'I fear you more than any spectre I have seen.'

Mr Murphy holds up his hand to stop me. 'Edie, wait up. You're just reading the words off a page.'

Duh, that's what he told me to do. Has he got a cheesing memory problem or something?

'You should be feeling the words,' he continues, getting up from his chair, and moving around the room in small paces, as if he has trapped wind! 'Imagine you're Ebenezer Scrooge.' Mr Murphy stops in his tracks and looks deeply serious. 'In one single night, you've not only seen the ghost of your old business partner, but you've also seen your past, your present, and now you're seeing your fourth ghost, your *future*. You're tired. It's been a long evening, you're starting to come to terms with the fact that you have made many mistakes in your life and you're now terrified to see what the future holds.'

I re-read the script in my head, now imagining what Scrooge had been through. It must've been quite the night. I feel a bit sorry for him. He's not a bad man; he's just grumpy and over time, he has got grumpier and grumpier because nobody has the guts to tell him to smile once in a while.

He reminds me of my Grandad Eric. I think about the story he told us when he came round for tea, the one where he chased the teenagers down his street with a broom.

Those teenagers probably think that my Grandad Eric is moody and mean, but he's not, he just likes having a clean garden. He's a little bit misunderstood, like Scrooge.

I imagine that I am Scrooge, frightened and alone, and I read the lines again.

'Ghost of the Future, I fear you more than any spectre I have seen. But, as I know your purpose is to do me good, and as I hope to live to be another man from what I was, I am prepared to bear you company, and do it with a thankful heart. Will you not speak to me?' I drop my voice on the last part; I'm eager, yet afraid of the answer.

I finish, and grin. I quite enjoyed that! I wait for what feels like a lifetime, but Mr Murphy doesn't say anything.

Well, this is totes awks. He's just sitting there in silence looking at me. I have no idea what he's thinking because his face is totally blank. Great, fab-u-lous, I've definitely ballsed it up.

Mr Murphy finally tears out a page from his notebook and writes something down. 'Thank you, Edie. Please be sure to check the drama noticeboard on Wednesday. The cast list will be up then.'

Ha! As if! He's being kind. There's no way my name will be on the board. No way, José.

Wednesday 8.55am

Ebenezer Scrooge – Edie Eckhart.

I look at the drama noticeboard again, reading that line over and over until it is imprinted on my brain. Is this some kind of sick joke? It's not very funny!

I feel someone behind me. I turn around and Mr Murphy is beaming at me.

'Congratulations, Edie. You're a natural actor, and you blew me away in the audition. Your performance was heartfelt and genuine.'

'But . . . but . . . look, sir, it's just, all I did was pretend to be my Grandad Eric,' I stutter.

'I'd like to meet this Eric someday, he sounds like a character!'

Yes, I think, *but not a character that I have to play on stage in front of everyone.*

Mr Murphy's expression softens. 'How about you take the rest of the week to think about it? Talk to your friends and family, and see what they think. I bet they'll have the best advice.'

'Okay, thanks Mr Murphy,' I say, walking away. My

mind is racing with the possibility of being a REAL
ACTOR! I can't work out if this is totally terrifying or
completely brilliant.

After school 3.45pm

'You pretended to be me?' Grandad Eric chuckles on our drive home. 'Well, I can't wait to see your performance of me on stage!'

'I haven't agreed to it yet, Grandad. I don't know if I will say yes. I mean, can I be an actor?'

'If Judi Dench can do it, then my Edie Eckhart can do it!'

'Yeah, but Judi Dench doesn't have cerebral palsy.'

We pull up outside my house, and Grandad Eric leans over and holds my hand. 'My granddaughter can do anything she puts her determined mind to, and never forget it!'

I smile and get out of the car. 'Thanks, Grandad Eric. Oh, Mum says you can stay for tea if you want.'

'What's she making?'

'Fishcakes.'

Grandad Eric puts his grumpy face on and shakes his head. 'No thanks, I'll stop off at the bakery on the way home and pick up a sausage roll for my supper!'

I must get my love for sausage rolls from him!

'Bye love, see you tomorrow!' Grandad Eric shouts and winds up the window, beeping his horn as his car rattles down the street.

Saturday 2.45pm

It's the weekend before I have to give Mr Murphy my final answer about the play and I still haven't made my decision.

I did what he suggested and asked my friends and family for advice.

Oscar told me to take the role, and to stop being such a scaredy-baby about it. He thinks that I will really like Mr Murphy when I get to know him better – apparently, he's 'multi-layered'. Oscar's changed his tune. I think 'multi-layered' is actually code for Mr Murphy allowing Oscar to sit next to Georgia in tutor group, so they get to hold hands under the table. Vomaccino.

Mum also thought I should take it.

'I think it's important to experience new things for personal growth. And it might be an opportunity to make new friends, love!' she said, when I asked her whether or not I should accept the part. Will she ever give the friends thing a rest?

My dad said, 'Absolutely yes, do it – but don't go too near the edge of the stage, because you might break a limb.' Which is a classic response from Steve 'Safety First' Eckhart.

Even though I don't know her *that* well, I wish I could ask Flora what she thinks. She would know what to do. I must remember to get her mobile number when I next see her.

'If you're still not sure, why don't you do one of your pros and cons lists? They normally help you decide what to do,' Mum suggests.

She does make a good point, and hopefully it'll help me come to a decision, so, here we go:

Pros

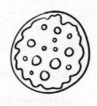

- Mr Murphy said that, in the final week of rehearsals, they rehearse and eat pizza. I like pizza.

- More potential to get to know more boys, and then find one nice enough to be my boyfriend. Like, surely boys who are actors are better than Oscar's suggestion of one from his football team . . .

- I like dressing up, and it would be very fun to dress like an old Victorian man!
- Rehearsals are on Mondays when Oscar now has football practice, so it's something to do when he's busy kicking a ball around.
- If Mr Murphy gets to know me he might let me write the next school play (who needs a mega-old Charles Dickens story when you have a soon-to-be-famous writer like Edie Eckhart at your school!).

Cons

- I might be a bad actor and everybody might laugh at me.

Even though there is only one thing on the con list, it is a pretty scary con. What if I am a bad actor? Mr Murphy gave me the role after seeing me act for literally one minute, hardly enough time for him to know whether I'd be good or not.

But there is the pizza. I LOVE pizza.

I'm going to really think about it tomorrow. I'll probably have a day off from writing in my diary, even if something cool happens, because I need to study my pros and cons list – I have to make the right decision and I don't have long!

Monday 5.53pm

Okay, guess who decided to listen to all her friends and family and accepted the role. That's right . . . ME!

And now here I am, at my first rehearsal of *A Christmas Carol*.

Mr Murphy has decided to kick the session off with what he describes as a 'fun yet educational game that will help us all get to know each other, and our bodies, better'. Everyone at rehearsal gives each other knowing looks when he says that because we can all tell from his tone that it is likely to be neither fun, nor educational. Plus I know how my body works – slowly, and not always in the way I want it to.

'Pretend you're a giraffe. That's it, move around the space. How do you walk? How do you hold yourself?'

I mean, honestly, how many giraffes are in *A Christmas Carol*? Oh yeah – a big, fat ZERO. Wouldn't it be better if we just cracked on with our lines?

But no, here we are.

Clearly, my giraffe still has cerebral palsy, because I am wobbling all over the hall – *Can giraffes even have CP?*

Halfway through the exercise I spy a girl at the other side of the room – I recognise her as one of Georgia's friends. I think her name is Poppy. She's concentrating super hard on stretching her neck as far as she can and wobbling on her tiptoes . . . it's so funny, I can't help but laugh! She clocks me laughing at her and laughs too, until we both have tears running down our cheeks from the laughing. Soon the whole group is laughing.

'All right, all right, all right, a herd of giggling giraffes wasn't *exactly* what I had in mind, but gather round, and let's introduce ourselves.'

We sit in a big circle, and Mr Murphy makes us tell each other our names, the roles we're playing and one interesting fact about ourselves. I sit next to Poppy, who is playing Mrs Cratchit. Poppy went to primary school in

Sweden. On my other side is Tom, who is playing Mr Cratchit. He loves football.

'Hello, I'm Edie, I'm playing Scrooge and I once ate eighteen pancakes in one sitting!'

Everybody seems genuinely impressed. The whole circle laughs.

'Woah! I once ate thirteen pancakes and I thought that was good! Respect!' Tom says.

I smile back. Maybe this won't be so bad after all. I'm actually having fun.

'And helping paint the set is Flora Ito.' Mr Murphy gestures towards the stage at the end.

YAY, Flora's here. What a win! Of course she's painting the set, because she's an amaaazing artist.

Flora pops her head out from behind the curtain. 'Hi,' she whispers quietly, almost talking to the floor. And then she's gone.

I smile to myself. In some ways, me and Flora are like the total opposite. I love meeting and chatting to new people and clearly she *hates* it.

Even though I only saw Flora for lits two seconds, I really liked seeing her and I'm hoping this means I'll get to see a lot more of her. It looks like I made the right decision saying yes to the play.

☆☆☆

After rehearsal, I have to wait for Oscar to finish football practice, so I decide to explore a bit.

I go into one of the side rooms and as soon as I walk in, someone shouts,

'BOO!' I'm so startled that I jump, wobble and my phone flies across the room.

It's Flora. What a stroke of luck! She's holding a paintbrush.

'Ohmigoodness I didn't see you there, Flora! You made me drop my phone. Can you pick it up?'

'No, Edie,' she says firmly. 'Sorry for making you jump, but you have two working arms, so *you* should pick it up.'

WHAT? I have cerebral palsy and she made me drop my phone. Of course she should pick it up. Nobody ever says 'no' to me. When I ask for help, people help me. That is what's supposed to happen when a disabled person asks.

She doesn't budge though, so I walk over, bend down and pick my phone up . . . and then eye-roll myself for essentially proving her point. I hate being proven wrong.

'Nice war wound!' Flora says, pointing to my chin and changing the subject. It's actually at the crusty, itchy stage, where all I want to do is pick off the chin scab. I keep having to stop myself from scratching it because the worst thing I could do right now is have a permanent scar to remind me of the first time I tried, and spectacularly failed, to ask Henry Witty out.

'Congratulations on getting the main part too,' Flora says. 'Although you smile too much to be Scrooge. I need to give you a few tips on how to frown!'

'And I can give you tips on how to turn that frown upside down!' That was a good one; I'm proud of that, to be honest. We laugh.

It is hard to stay annoyed with Flora about the phone thing. 'It was nice seeing you in rehearsal, even though it was for two seconds. You couldn't disappear quick enough!' I tease. 'You didn't even share an interesting fact about yourself.'

'I hate group situations like that,' she admits. 'But if I had to do it, I would probably say . . .' she stands to attention, and puts on a loud, serious voice. 'Hello, my name is Flora Ito, I am doing set design and I have seen every episode of *The Simpsons* five times, at least.'

'FIVE TIMES? Wow, that's impressive!'

'It's an obsession,' Flora admits. She picks up her paintbrush again and begins painting, her tongue sticking out in concentration as she works on the detailed bits.

I take a seat. 'I'm waiting for my friend Oscar to walk home with. Do you mind if I sit with you? I won't disturb you, promise!'

Flora smiles. 'Of course, that's totally fine. It's nice to have your company. I might not talk much, though. I'm in "the zone" and I've almost finished the back board for the set.'

I unzip my backpack and take out my comic: *True Believers: The Amazing Spider-Man.*

Flora puts her paintbrush down immediately and

starts talking a million words a minute. 'Marvel girl, are you? I like DC more, although I really like this Spider-Man series. It's really good, isn't it? I've been saving up to buy that one!'

Okay, this is legit amazing. I can't believe Flora is into comics. She is absolutely and completely friend material!

'You can borrow it when I've read it, if you'd like,' I say, although it's a big deal for me to let anyone touch my comics . . . because of the time Oscar read one of my favourites whilst eating a jam sandwich, and when he gave it back, all the pages were stuck together.

For the first time since I've known her, Flora smiles so wide, I can see all the train track braces on her teeth. 'I'd love that!' She looks really cute.

☆☆☆

On our walk home, I find myself going on and on to Oscar about rehearsal, but Oscar seems up for hearing it all. Anyway, he owes me, because I spend a lot of time hearing about football these days.

Oscar obvs finds the giraffe task we had to do

hilarious. He lets go of my arm and starts running around on his tiptoes.

'You look exactly like Poppy!' I say. 'She was such a funny giraffe!'

He stretches out his neck to reach a low-hanging leaf on a tree and pulls it down with his teeth, pretending to eat it. Immediately, he pulls the leaf out of his mouth and throws it on the floor.

'Ewww, I think that leaf had bird poo on it!' He spits out some leaf on the ground and frowns. 'RANK!' he bellows. It's got white bits on it. I laugh until I think I'm going to wee myself.

I can't wait for Oscar to meet my clever, funny, talented, serious new friend Flora. She's not like anybody I know in the world.

Tuesday 4.10pm

LOUIE HAS BROKEN HIS ARM!

I am majorly worried about him. Mum texted me
from the hospital. Apparently, after school, Mum
took him to a playground, and
he got way too excited on
the climbing frame and fell
on his arm funny. Mum said
she literally heard his bone go
crack! GROSS.

He's all right though. Obviously he cried a lot when
he did it, but now they're in A&E and he's got a lolly and
a sticker, so he just thinks it's a nice day out.

Mum asked if I'd be okay on my own at home for a
bit while they put Louie's arm in a cast – Dad's at work,
and Grandad Eric is at his bridge club. I told her of
course, because that way I have loads of alone time to
practise my lines!

I now have a script, which is super mega thick.
There's no way I can learn all these lines. No way, José!
Mr Murphy said the more I practise, the easier it will

become, but I am not convinced. Surely my eleven-year-old brain is not big enough for all these words! But all I can do is try, so here goes . . .

I sit on my bed, eating Jaffa Cakes. In between mouthfuls, I read out loud. 'If I could work my will, every idiot who goes about with "Merry Christmas" on his lips, should be boiled with his own pudding, and buried with a stake of holly through his heart. He should!'

That's one of the lines I've got to remember for my role as Scrooge. I furrow my eyebrows and give a moody scowl, doing my best impression of Scrooge (Grandad Eric!). I'm starting to realise it's going to be pretty fun playing an old, grumpy man.

'Bah! Humbug!' is another thing Scrooge says a lot. I've got Dickens to thank for that. It's basically what I plan to say to anyone who asks me a question. 'Edie, do you want to help me do the washing up?' Mum will ask, and I can legit reply 'Bah! Humbug!' It's great. Sure, Scrooge was a bad-tempered man, but at least he got out of doing boring household chores.

Thursday 4.48pm

It's cold, I'm outside and somebody needs to explain the concept of football to me, because from where I'm standing it's just a load of people kicking and chasing a ball around a field. I mean, how is that fun?

I'm trying to be a good friend and support Oscar (and get free hot chocolate at half time), and to be fair, he is better than I expected. I thought he'd spend the whole time face down in the mud, but he's only fallen over once . . . so far!

My ears are ringing because every time Oscar gets control of the ball, Georgia screams – she is a much more supportive supporter than me. She also understands the rules. Every so often she yells 'REF! OFFSIDE!' and I've got lits no idea what she's on about.

'Oi, Edie, mate,' Oscar shouts across the field, 'I just scored a goal and you weren't even watching!'

I don't think he can hear me because it's suddenly very windy, but I shout back, 'I was too. I saw you kick that ball in the net. Well done. Good kicking!'

Georgia laughs. 'Nice one!' She's actually been really friendly recently, and she's stopped saying silly things

about my disability. It's like she's completely forgotten that I am disabled at all.

'So Edie, do you fancy any of the boys on the football team?' She's teamed up with Oscar to head up the 'Get Edie A Boyfriend' club, and she's taking the job *very* seriously.

'Not really,' I admitted. 'I don't know a lot of them, but let's be real, they all have something the matter with them.'

1. **JACK – TOO TALL**
2. **HARRY K – SMELLS OF CHEESE**
3. **MO – TOO MOODY**
4. **LUKAS – ALREADY GOT A GIRLFRIEND**
5. **JAYDEN – OBSESSED WITH HIMSELF**
6. **REECE – BAD GUY, NOPE**
7. **BOBBY – MAAYYYYBEE**
8. **OSCAR – JUST NO HAHAHAHA**
9. **TOBY – GAY**
10. **HAZ – MAYYYYYBEEE**
11. **HARRY B – ALREADY GOT A GIRLFRIEND**

I think about my list. 'Apart from Bobby or Haz I suppose. They're both in my tutor group and we've chatted a few times.'

Georgia leans closer. 'OMG, Edie. WHAT a coincidence.' Georgia points over at the field. 'Bobby is totally looking at you!' She is right, Bobby is totally smiling at ME! This is unreal.

We watched the rest of the match, but to be honest nothing majorly exciting happened. The ball was kicked, goals were scored, HOT CHOCOLATES were consumed. Me and Georgia had three each, then the sugar went to our heads and we kept laughing at Oscar. He was trying sooo hard. And he kept looking over at us for encouragement holding his thumbs up, which for some reason was very funny, and made us laugh even more.

Even though I like comics and Georgia likes make-up, we had a really nice afternoon talking about boys and laughing at Osc. She even invited me to a sleepover in a few weeks' time. I am Excited with a capital E!

Monday 3.48pm

Flora's here at rehearsal already, in her secret side room. The single Victorian house has turned into a whole street. It's dead impressive.

I can hear everyone in the hall singing 'fa-la-laaaa' to warm up their voice muscles. I'll have to be quick, rehearsal officially starts in ten minutes.

'BOO!' I yell, from behind the door.

She doesn't even flinch, but she laughs as she looks up. 'Nice try, Eckhart!'

I pull my comic out of my bag and walk into the room. 'I've finished reading *Spider-Man*, if you still want to borrow it?'

Flora drops her paintbrush and rubs her hands on her already paint-covered rainbow  dungarees, before rushing over to me.

'Yes please!' she says excitedly. 'What's your number? I'll text you when I've read it. Mind you, I'm not a big texter.' That doesn't surprise me – Flora not being a big talker or a big texter. She's just a quiet artist. We really could not be more different.

Flora puts her number in my phone and I give her the comic. Flora holds it carefully, as if it's made out of gold and diamonds and is the most precious thing in the world. It's the correct response.

'Amazing,' she says. 'Thank you so much, I'll give it back to you as soon as I've read it.'

'No rush!' I say, trying to sound as cool as a cucumber. I know Flora will take good care of my book, but it's still hard handing it over. It's one of my babies!

'I've actually brought something for you. Now, it's DC, but hear me out . . .' Flora handed me a tatty comic.

'DC is rubbish!' I say, only half joking.

'Honestly, this one will change your mind,' she explains. 'I got it from a charity shop. I prefer second-hand comics. I like to imagine where the comics have been before I get them, it's like they've been on their own journey.'

I nod, speechless at the front cover of *Oracle: The Cure*.

'Thank you!' I manage, fascinated by the illustration on the front.

'I know your disability isn't everything, but when we first met and talked, it made me think,' Flora goes on. 'And I got angry that there's virtually no disabled characters in comic books, when disability should be represented like everything else. It's just a bit frustrating that even in today's society, we can't see people we relate to on TV, or in comic books.

'Like, take me, my mum's parents are Japanese, my dad is white. I know I wouldn't change who I am, but you know, it'd be nice to have someone who looks a bit like me portrayed as a superhero, just once!

'This is the first book in a three-part series, so if you like this one just let me know, and you can borrow the other two. The main character is Barbara Gordon, who used to be Batgirl, but in this series, she's a wheelchair user.'

Flora pauses for air. 'I'm sorry,' she says. 'My mum says it's all or nothing with me. I either don't say anything or you can't shut me up!'

I laugh. 'But you're right.' I frown. 'There's barely *any* disabled characters in the Marvel comics. And certainly nobody who remotely looks or sounds like me, which is a bit gutting.'

Flora looks thoughtful. I carry on talking. 'Even though I like being disabled, it is hard when there's nobody like me that I can look up to. It makes me wonder if I'm doing it right. Is there a correct way to be a disabled pre-teen? I dunno.'

Flora laughs. 'I think you're doing all right. Although you should stop being so lazy and pick up your own phone when you drop it!'

I nod. UGH she's right. I hate being wrong!

'You know when we met at the party, you asked me whether I thought that I would be different, if I wasn't disabled,' I say.

Flora nods.

'I think I would be different, but maybe not in a good way. Being disabled makes me appreciate all the great things in life and it makes me focus on them, instead of getting down about the rubbish stuff. I like to focus on what I can do, rather than what I can't do. I don't have the skills to tie my shoelaces at a super fast speed, but I do have a great family, I'm happy, I'm healthy and I have a brilliant life. I feel lucky to be me. Does that make sense?'

'Yeah,' Flora says, smiling. 'That makes complete sense! I love how positive you are.'

I thank Flora for the comic and promise to give it back as soon as I've read it, probably after half term. She smiles, and gets back to painting the set, while I head out to do my fa-la-las with the rest of the cast.

☆☆☆

I really enjoyed rehearsal today. We practised the beginning of the play, which was fun because I could be peak Grandad Eric.

Mr Murphy was clearly having a 'yellow day'. He wandered into the school hall in yellow trousers and a yellow tie. I'm surprised he wasn't wearing yellow shoes too!

Poppy wasn't in many scenes today, but she watched a lot of it, sitting next to Mr Murphy, giving her own notes, and shouting, 'Bravo!' whenever I did one of my big speeches.

'Am I the assistant director, sir?' she asked Mr Murphy at the end of rehearsal.

'You're a pest, Poppy Lennox, that's what you are!' he said. But you could see that Mr Murphy was a little bit tickled by her.

Before we left rehearsal, Mr Murphy gave us a big

target – in three weeks, after half term, we should all be 'off-book'. That meant we should all know our lines by heart, without needing to look at the script. Which is easy for somebody like Poppy, who has like four lines in the whole play, but how am I meant to remember all of mine? I have literally thousands of words to remember.

Now I'm waiting for Oscar, so we can walk home together. I'm sitting here watching him finish up his football game, which is Dullsville, Alabama. He's actually getting quite good. He just scored a mega goal, but I won't tell him that, otherwise he'll get an even bigger head than he already has.

Now, oh great, here's Oscar, time to go, woo-hoo! Oh, no, wait, his friend Bobby is coming over WITH him. What does he want? I breathe on my hand and inhale to check my breath sitch – mint chocolate fresh!

'Hiya Edie! We were just talking about you!' Oscar says excitedly. 'This is Bobby.'

'I know who he is, Oscar, jeeeeez. Hey Bob,' I say confidently, smiling at him.

Bobby smiles and goes bright red. 'How are you, Edie Eckhart?' he asks.

Bobby

I think he has a bit of a lisp, which I like, because that means we both sound a bit funny! It's also hilarious he addressed me by my entire name. Totally formal and uncool in quite a cute way.

Oscar sits next to me and pats the bench. Bobby sits down awkwardly. Then Oscar jumps up, moving to the other side of me, so Bobby is sitting NEXT to me. He's such a joker sometimes, and loves making me feel embarrassed. I make a mental note to get back at him later.

After we chat for a while on the bench, the three of us walk home together, talking about what we're going to do on Halloween. Bobby is taking his sister trick-or-treating. 'What will you do?' Bobby asks, turning to me.

'We're going to carve pumpkins, but I don't think anybody trusts *these* hands with a carving knife!' I wobble my hands and Oscar and Bobby laugh.

Oscar turns up the street to go on to his house, yelling, 'See ya later, you two!' He CLEARLY wanted to give me and Bobby time to talk on our own. I know what he's playing at.

After a few minutes of totes awkward silence, Bobby says, 'Oscar said you're coming to watch his next football game after half term?'

I nod. 'Yeah, but honestly, I have no idea what's happening. I just come for the hotdogs!'

Bobby smiles shyly. 'Don't tell Oscar, or any of the boys on the team, but eating hotdogs is my favourite part too. Maybe we can go for a hotdog together, after the match?'

I nod, feeling super-duper excited.

'Great!' Bobby grins. 'Please can I give you my number?'

I nod – seriously, have I lost the ability to speak? – and I hand him my phone.

Is this really happening? This is *amazing*!

This is not a drill, I HAVE A DATE. Actually, this is terrifying. I've only seen dates in films. Do we order a milkshake with two straws? What happens if I want my own milkshake? What if he's lactose intolerant?

I HAVE A DATE AFTER HALF TERM!!!

Friday 6.15pm

It's four days later and I'm still thinking about the conversation I had with Flora about comics and disability. Well that, and another, more pressing matter. In case you didn't know, I HAVE A DATE.

Obviously, I read *The Oracle* immediately in one sitting, from front to back. It was brilliant. Even though the main character, Barbara, is a wheelchair user, it doesn't stop her from doing all the things she wants to do, and it's made me think harder about my disability. I've never let it stop me from doing all the things I want to do, but maybe sometimes I use it as an excuse. Like, imagine if Mr Murphy had accepted the Card, and believed that just because I'm disabled, I can't be an actor – then I wouldn't be Scrooge. I LOVE being Scrooge. I'm starting to think I was born to play him. Who knew I was born to play a grumpy old man?

I message Flora.

> Hey Flora, it's Edie from school ☺ LOVED Oracle SO MUCH. Are you enjoying Spider-Man? Hopefully see you soon

I sit on my bed and think. After the chats I've had with Flora, it feels like for the first time in my life I'm considering my disability and where I fit in a world where most people around me aren't disabled. It's exciting and scary at the same time.

And it's quite a lot to think about when you are only eleven! Anyway, today it's the last day of school before half term. I'm going to miss school next week. Hanging out with Flora, chatting more to Georgia, Poppy, Mrs Adler, and even (dare I say it) Mr Murphy too!

October Half Term. Monday 2.04pm

Today is a great day! This half term has got off to a cracking start. Although I do miss rehearsals. I even miss pretending that I'm a giraffe once a week.

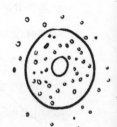

I've spent the whole day with just Oscar. No Georgia, no parents and not even Charlie. Mum dropped us off in town, and we mooched around all day. Oscar bought a new black and white stripy beanie and I bought yellow laces for my Converse . . . fancy! Now we've bought hot doughnuts from the stand and we're eating them on the beach, watching dogs playing in the sea.

October is my favourite time of the year, because there aren't any stupid tourists barging through town, and as long as you wrap up, it's brilliant to be outside in the fresh air, especially when you warm up your insides with hot sugary doughnuts!

'You have sugar on your face,' Oscar says, leaning over with a napkin.

'Don't worry, my friend,' I pull out a wad of tissues from my dunga dress pocket. 'I brought all the napkins I will ever need.'

I love Osc, and how much he cares about me, but maybe Mrs Adler (and Flora) are right. I should pick up my own phone when I drop it and I should wipe up my own face when it's got sugar on it.

We talk a bit about my upcoming date with Bobby, but we decide date chat is legit Boring with a capital B.

'Hangman?' Oscar asks.

'Yeah, thought you'd never ask!'

Oscar laughs, guessing the hangman almost immediately. 'Edie! You're obsessed with the play!'

He's right, but I don't think that's a bad thing. I've finally found something I might be good at. And it's something that I am doing for myself, and that makes me happy. I take a giant bite of my doughnut to celebrate.

Wednesday 6.10am

I AM SO EXCITED. Even though it's WAY too early for me to be up. Seriously, I don't think the birds are even awake at this time.

Every October half term me, Louie and Dad go on a camping trip to Whitby. Mum goes on her 'Gals' Weekend Away' to Leeds (where her and her friends drink loads of rosé wine and talk about how much they fancy the dancers in *Strictly Come Dancing*) and the 'Lads' (Dad, Louie and me) pop off to Whitby.

We're on our way there in the car, as I write.

Dad is an amazing dad, but he's at work a lot of the time, so this is a good chance for me and Louie to hang out with him, and as Dad says, spend some 'quality time' together.

Whitby is only up the road from us, but it still feels like a proper holiday. I love staying in a tent and cosying up in my sleeping bag, snug as a bug in a rug. I can't wait to blow up my airbed. I like to pretend that I'm a survival expert, like Bear Grylls – but hopefully I won't have to drink my own wee!

'Didi!' Louie nudges my arm. 'Stop writing and play I Spy with me. I'll go first. I spy with my little eye, something beginning with . . . C!'

I know the answer. 'Cast?' I say.

He nods. Louie, ever the optimist, is happy that he broke his arm because it meant all his new friends at school signed his cast. Plus, all the adults have been calling him a brave boy.

Dad

'You're such a brave boy,' Dad says now, on cue, looking emotional in the rear-view mirror. 'Isn't he brave, Edie?'

'Yes, SO brave!' I kiss his head.

'My arm isn't working right now, just like yours, Edie!' he says, beaming. I wish more people were like Louie. He doesn't see my disability as a bad thing; he just sees his big sister Edie. He's happy when he breaks his arm,

because it means he can be more like me.

'Didi, the doctor said that my arm will be better in six weeks when the bones are mended. When will your arms be better?'

I tell him that my arms will never be mended, this is just how my arms are, and Louie looks sad.

'It's not a bad thing though, Lou, it's just something that makes me, me. Like, I have brown eyes, and you have blue eyes. I have wobbly hands and you don't.'

Louie reaches across the car with his free arm and holds my hand. 'I like your wobbly hands.'

Thursday 3.32pm

Camping is a real adventure. Last night, there was an owl right outside my tent, it lulled me to sleep with its twit-twoos. I even saw bats. The only downside is the rubbish phone signal.

This morning, I decided to climb on the camping table to try and get some bars of signal. You always see it in movies – like holding your phone to the sky, and being closer to space, will make the messages fly through the air and land in your phone. But in case you're about to try it – don't. It doesn't work.

'Get down from there, Edie!' Dad said, on his way back from the showers, juggling the shampoo, body wash bottles and towels. 'I don't want two children with broken arms, thank you very much!' *Such a Dad thing to say!*

TO: OSCAR

> Camping's great, but the signal's rubbish. Are you having a nice week? Back on Friday ☺
>
> **UNSENT**

In the end I gave up and put my phone back in my bag. Dad says I should have a 'digital detox' anyway, which means no phones and no iPads. Apparently we should be at one with nature, before we get back to our normal lives. This afternoon we are going crabbing and tomorrow we are going on a fishing trip, and I can't wait – I haven't been fishing before. I hope it's fun!

Friday 5.25pm

Fishing is not fun. According to Dad, I don't have 'sea legs'. I should've known – my land legs aren't very good either.

Whilst I spewed my guts up into a paper bag, Louie and my dad had a great time. Louie caught a mackerel that was bigger than his head!

We're in the car going back home. I'm gutted to be leaving so soon – it feels like we've only just got here!

Louie is excited to see Mum, and to tell her about the fish he caught and also that 'Didi was sick everywhere', which he finds hilarious.

Now that I'm back in civilisation, I finally have phone signal. I'm expecting to get lots of texts from Oscar, but nothing appears. It's a bit odd, because usually we talk every day.

Finally, my phone vibrates. Thank banana for that! But it's not Oscar.

FLORA

Really happy you liked the comic ☺. I'm LOVING Spider-Man too. How's your half term? Are you free to do something on Saturday?

My heart feels fluttery. I've been hoping Flora is my new friend, but this feels like proof. I reply immediately.

> Glad to hear it. Sounds great, my half term is good so far, although I realised that I am not meant to be a fisherman

'Didi, why are you smiling?' Louie asks me. 'Are you thinking about you being sick again?'

He falls about laughing. It's a good job I love him so much and he's so cute, Also, I can't help but smile, smile, smile. I'm going to see Flora outside of school. Get in!

Saturday 8.32am

'Didi, look, I'm eating Hula Hoops!'

We've gone swimming, but because of Louie's cast, he can't go in the pool. Mum and Dad were worried that he would feel left out, but actually he's perfectly happy to sit by the side of the pool with Mum, eating crisps.

Dad is teaching me how to swim. It's a bit embarrassing to admit that I'm nearly twelve and I still can't swim, but I'm getting there, slowly. I just need to make sure that my arms and my legs do what I tell them to, when I tell them to, which isn't so straightforward when you have cerebral palsy. They honestly have a mind of their own!

'That's it Edie, careful, focus on your breathing.' Dad is walking by the side of me, ready to swoop in if I suddenly go under. But I don't! I make it to the other side, without even stopping!

Mum and Louie cheer me on from the side of the pool. Louie walks up to me and carefully pops a crisp in my mouth. 'Well done, Didi. I love you.'

Evening

I'm still on a high after my swimming breakthrough this morning. Paralympics, here I come! And now it's time to go and meet Flora.

'Oooh, you look nice,' says Mum when I come downstairs.

I'm wearing my Converse (with my new yellow laces) and a purple, stripy dungaree dress. 'Thanks, Ma!'

'You take care of yourself, won't you?' Mum says. She worries about me and my wobbles, but she has always let me do all the things that other people my age can do. She can be annoying, and nag me, but she has never stopped me from being just like everybody else. I would *never* admit this to her, but she is quite a decent mum really.

'Yes, Mum,' I say.

'And give Oscar my love, won't you,' she adds, as we walk down the hall.

'I'm not meeting Oscar, Mum. I'm meeting my new friend, Flora!'

Mum looks surprised. 'Oh! What's this Flora like?'

I shrug, not really knowing how to explain Flora.

'She's cool. And funny. A bit shy. She wants to be an illustrator when she's older.'

Mum puts her thumbs up, as if she approves.

'Okay, well, look after yourself. You're just going to the cinema?'

I nod. 'We're going to see the latest Pixar film, which I know we're a bit old for, but really, everyone loves Pixar. And maybe we'll go to the arcades for a bit after.'

'Sounds like a plan, have fun, mushroom! Text me when the film ends and I'll come and pick you up.'

'Thanks, bye Mum!'

It must be the lighting, but when I look back Mum looks a bit tearful, even though she's smiling her big Mum smile. I don't know what that's all about.

☆☆☆

When I see Flora inside the cinema building, she looks legit cool in her black dungarees, red and white stripy top and a black beanie. She's holding her skateboard. She runs up to me and gives me a giant hug – I think it's the first hug we've ever had, and it's really nice!

'Okay,' she says, pulling away. 'Big question for you . . . what's your popcorn flavour of choice? Sweet, like you?'

I can't help but laugh. 'I am very sweet, it's true. Okay, here goes. Hear me out . . . I like sweet AND salty! It's like Christmas because you don't know what you're going to get, it's all about the surprise!'

Flora doesn't look convinced. 'Fine, but we're getting Minstrels and putting them in the popcorn too!'

I think this is the moment – above the comic books and the coolness that radiates

130

from Flora – that I realise she has true best friend potential. Chocolate and sweet and salty popcorn together. What a combination! WINNING!

☆☆☆

The film was Great with a capital G. It even made me cry at the end, which I thought was super lame and embarrassing, until I looked at Flora, and she was wiping a tear from her eye too.

When we come out into the foyer, we realise that

despite our best efforts we still have a load of Minstrels and popcorn left.

But the really cool thing about Bridlington is that the cinema is directly opposite the beach, and all the

benches outside it look out to sea. 'We could sit outside and finish the box?' I suggest.

Flora nods, looking super happy with my suggestion.

We choose the bench in the middle. It's turned dark while we've been in the film and the moon reflects in the water. It's Awesome with a capital A. As I sit down and swing my backpack off my shoulder, my diary falls out.

'Every time I see you at school, you're writing in that thing,' Flora says. 'Concentrating with your tongue out.'

I laugh, picking my diary up from the pavement. 'I didn't realise my tongue comes out when I concentrate!' I remember Flora painting scenery; she did the same. 'It's just my diary. I write about my day and people I meet and stuff like that.'

Do you ever write about me?' Flora asks, looking slightly nervous.

I nod, suddenly aware that I write about Flora *a lot*. I

don't want to scare my new friend away by telling her exactly how much!'

She asks about my family and I tell her about Louie, and the story about me spewing on the fishing trip and how hilarious he found it.

'He sounds right cheeky!' she says.

I smile. 'Oh, he is, and I think he's only going to get even cheekier as he grows up. I'm properly dreading the day he gets taller than me!'

'Aww but I bet he's going to protect his big sister!' Flora says, and then she tells me about her family too. Flora doesn't know her dad, he left when she was little, and she doesn't have any brothers or sisters. But when she talks about her mum, Sara, who I *heard* at Georgia's party, her whole face lights up.

Sara sounds brilliant. According to Flora, 'she's got a personality as big as her laugh!' (which, if I remember correctly from the party, is MASSIVE). She's got something called MS, which stands for multiple sclerosis. MS means she has trouble walking, and her disability is getting worse and worse.

Flora tells me she's her mum's carer, which means

that she bathes her, dresses her and cooks for her. Most days, they also get help in from a nurse.

We don't talk for a while after Flora finishes telling me about her mum. Instead, Flora gets out her sketchbook and a pencil and starts drawing.

We've only been out of the film for a little while. Have we already run out of things to talk about? Maybe I'm a really boring friend and that's why Oscar prefers spending time with Georgia.

Well, there's no time like the present. If Flora's sketching, I'm going to write in my diary.

I write and Flora draws. Finally, Flora says, 'It's not perfect, but what do you think?'

She holds up her sketchbook. She has drawn a superhero girl with a cape, Converse and a small rip in one of her tights. In one hand she holds a book, and in the other, a pen.

It is completely Brilliant with a capital B! 'She looks cool! Is she a DC character? I don't think I know her.'

Flora laughs, shaking her head. She rips out the page from her book and hands it to me. I stare at it, frowning. I still don't get it.

'Edie, it's you!'

I look again, and I see it. It *is* me! I just didn't recognise me at first because Flora has turned me into a superhero.

Flora nudges me. 'You said you were annoyed that there weren't enough disabled characters in comics, so I thought I'd start to change that!'

I can't speak, and Flora looks worried. 'Do you hate it?'

I don't hate it at all – I love it so much, but I don't know how to put it into words. Not only is it an amazing drawing, but it's also personal to me. No one has ever made me into a superhero character before.

I'm about to thank her, but at that moment, Flora gets up from the bench. 'Sorry, I'd better get going. Mum gets worried if I stay out too late. Is your mum picking you up?'

I can see Mum's red car approaching out of the corner of my eye. 'Yes, she's just there. Listen, Flora . . .'

But before I can thank her for the picture, or even say goodbye, she's gone, skateboarding away at speed.

'Did you have a nice time with Flo?' Mum asks, as soon as I get in the car.

'Flora! Yeah, I really did! But she's not much of a talker.'

'That's all right. I bet you talk enough for the both of you,' she jokes, poking my side so much it tickled.

That's probably true, but I definitely should have told her how much I love her drawing of me. It was just so good, I didn't know what to say. I think about texting her, but I probably need to thank her properly in person.

Now we're home, I can't stop looking at the drawing. It really is properly amazing. I'm gonna stick it in my diary where I can look at it all day.

31st October 5.35pm

HAPPY HALLOWEEN!!

Today is a great day, because it's the one day in the year my parents let me loose with a carving knife!

We're not going trick-or-treating tonight. Me and Oscar have decided we're too old for that. It's all right for Bobby because he's got a little sister to take, so he can pretend he's doing it for her, when really it's obviously an excuse to get loads of sweets.

Louie's going with his best friend Ralph and his mum. It was so cute, earlier. Louie and Ralph were dressed as matching ghosts. I had to pretend to be really scared when they said 'Ooooooh', even though they just looked adorable.

Anyway, now Louie's gone out, me and Oscar decide to carve pumpkins and watch scary films. Well, actually we're going to watch *Hocus Pocus* and *Beetlejuice*. WINNING!

138

We've still dressed up, obvs, just for the lols. Oscar is a mummy (which is funny because he has bandages everywhere, including his mouth!) and I'm dressed like a vampire bride. We look *seriously* cool. I keep checking myself in the mirror. It's a look!

'Hey, Edie,' Oscar says, getting his phone out and turning on selfie mode. 'Do I look kinda good? I'm gonna send Georgia a selfie.'

'You do you, Osc,' I say, hacking at the pumpkin.

'Careful Edie,' Dad warns. He's standing over me at the living room table. He flinches every time he thinks my knife is remotely close to my hand.

'Honestly Dad, the more you scream, the more likely it is that I will *actually* chop my hand off.'

'Hey Mr E!' Oscar mumbles from under his bandages. He puts his phone down and starts carving a triangle for an eye. 'At least if Edie *does* chop her own hand off, you can stitch it back on!'

Dad raises his eyebrows. 'I don't actually specialise in reattaching children's hands, Oscar,' he says. 'Seriously Edie, that knife is deceptively sharp.'

'Of course it's sharp, Dad. It's a knife.' Honestly!

Dad takes a deep breath and heads off to the kitchen to cook tea.

'Are you looking forward to your date with Bobby on Thursday?' Oscar asks when Dad's out of earshot.

I can't be bothered to reply and talk about my date with Bobby, which I'm secretly a bit nervous about, so instead I take some pumpkin mulch and throw it at Osc. And we end up having a pumpkin mulch fight. It's awesome.

Monday 8.15pm

School was really great today. Over the holidays, I realised how much I missed it.

It was so good to be back and to see Mrs Adler. She has grown even bigger during half term. Honestly, her babies must be MASSIVE. She looked very nice today; she was wearing a bright red blouse and a big chunky necklace. I think I'll dress like Mrs Adler when I'm older; she has the best taste in clothes and always wears the brightest blouses.

We're in November, can you believe? Mr Murphy is getting stressed about the play so now we do TWO days of rehearsals a week, which is fine by me, because I love them.

All the other people in the show are very funny and I love getting to know them more, especially Poppy and Tom, so any excuse to spend more time with them sounds just brilliant. I'm even starting to enjoy Mr Murphy's silly warming-up exercises.

Today, we all had to curl up into a ball on the floor, and pretend we were being born. We wormed and stretched all over the hall, as we learnt how to walk and talk, until we were our regular selves just chatting to each other.

'Hello, my name is Poppy and I was born two minutes ago!'

'Pleased to meet you, Poppy; I'm Edie and I was born two minutes ago too!'

When we were all warmed up, we practised the last scene, where Scrooge, who is now a happy, jolly 'changed man', buys a turkey for the Cratchit family. Playing a jolly old man comes easier to me than playing a moody old man, so I really got into it.

'I will honour Christmas in my heart, and try to keep it all the year. I will live in the Past, the Present, and the Future. The Spirits of all Three shall strive within me. I will not shut out the lessons that they teach.'

I declared my final line as loud and as proud as I could, and everybody cheered.

Mr Murphy clapped along and *almost* smiled. 'Well, Eckhart, if you put on a performance like that in five weeks' time, I think this is going to be a jolly good show!'

'You're literally amaze, Edie! Born to be a star!' Poppy grinned, as she helped me down from the stage. 'Are you going to Georgia's sleepover at the weekend?'

Look at me! Edie Eckhart, making friends all over the place! Piece of cake!

I nod and Poppy gives me a big, tight bear hug. 'Great! I'll see you there.'

The only weird thing that happened was that I was going to go over to Flora to thank her for the drawing, but as I approached her, she put her headphones on like she didn't want to be disturbed, and she left as soon as we'd finished rehearsing. I hope I haven't done something to upset her.

Thursday 6.44pm (AKA THE DATE!)

I am halfway through the date with Bobby and, so far, so good!

The match was . . . well, it was football. Balls were kicked, goals were scored, yada, yada. You know the deal.

During the game, I stood with Georgia, and we chatted about half term. Apparently, she hung out with Oscar every day, which explains why I didn't hear from him much when I was camping.

'He kept wanting to watch superhero movies,' she said. 'But they're all the same, you know what I mean?'

'Yeah,' I agreed, but secretly I had no idea what she was going on about.

After the game had finished, me and Bobby got hotdogs from the stand and now we're eating them in the park. He's just gone to get us some drinks.

It's nice. I don't really know how you're supposed to act on a date, but we are talking a lot and he keeps laughing at my jokes, which feels like a good sign. It's really just like hanging out with Oscar – if Oscar was white, had floppy hair and a lisp!

I haven't got butterflies though. People always talk about butterflies in your belly when you meet someone you really fancy, don't they? All I have right now in my belly is nachos and hotdogs, which is probably better than butterflies anyway! Am I right?

Monday 5.40pm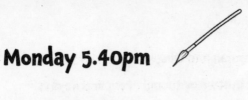

After rehearsal today, I pluck up the courage to go and talk to Flora. I can see she's painting the roofs of the houses, listening to her headphones.

'Hey, Flora!' I shout loudly as I approach, so she can hear me over her music. 'I had a great time at the cinema with you. Thank you so much for the drawing. I love it so much that it has taken pride of place in my diary so I can look at it whenever I like throughout the day.'

'You're welcome, Edie.' Flora looks back down at the set and dips her paintbrush in forest green paint. 'I saw you on Thursday, with a boy after school.'

'Oh, yeah, that was Bobby. Why didn't you come and say hello?'

'I was playing football.'

I didn't know Flora played football. I didn't even know Flora *liked* football. I mean, there's so many things I don't know about her. She's obviously what my dad would call 'multi-talented'.

'Why did you never mention football before? You could've taught me the rules! I've got no cheesing clue what's happening most of the time when I watch Oscar's matches. They run up and down and up and down, and at the end, one team is happy and one team is sad. I swear every match is exactly the same!'

Flora laughs. 'I can teach you the rules,' she says. 'I didn't mention it because . . . well, I don't really like talking about myself. I'm worried that I'm a bit boring.'

I want to tell her that she is the least boring person I have ever met and that I think she is wonderful and super-duper interesting, but I am also scared that she might run away again like she did after the cinema.

'I've still got some bits to paint, if you fancy joining me?' Flora points to a big piece of wood. When I paint, it usually goes *everywhere*, but this looks perfect for me. I grin at her and grab a brush. We don't talk, we paint.

Saturday 8.10pm

I'm at Georgia's sleepover and it's so much fun! All the girls, Poppy, Pip, Georgia and Chloe, are being super friendly, even though I'm the new one in the group. We've just watched a funny film, and now we're painting our nails and drinking hot chocolate.

I think back to my date with Bobby. It was really nice. I hope he asks me to be his girlfriend. So far, I haven't heard from him, like, at all. Fingers crossed he messages me soon.

Poppy is painting my nails gold with black lightning bolts, and telling everybody about the play. She's a very good multitasker.

'And then right at the end Edie, I mean Scrooge, is a changed person, so he comes round to the Cratchits with a big turkey!'

'Aw, Edie, Poppy, can you give us a sneak peek of the play?' Chloe asks.

Me and Poppy don't need *any* encouragement to show off, so we jump up, and wave our nails dry.

'Wait, I need a turkey!' I say.

'I have a packet of wafer-thin ham in the fridge. Will that work?' Georgia asks, very seriously.

'That'll do the job.'

Once Georgia has come back upstairs and handed me the packet of ham (luckily still closed), I clear my throat and begin.

'A merrier Christmas, Bob, my good fellow, than I have given you for many a year! I'll raise your salary, and endeavour to assist your struggling family, and we will discuss your affairs this very afternoon, over a Christmas bowl of *wafer thin ham*, Bob!'

Poppy puts on her mumsy Mrs Cratchit voice. 'God bless you, Mr Scrooge. The Founder of the Feast indeed!'

The girls cheer, and me and Poppy hold hands and bow, as if we're in a proper big theatre. Afterwards, we realise we're getting pretty hungry, so we crack open the ham and pass it round. Hot choc and ham – a winning combo. Who knew?

My phone buzzes.

BOBBY

Hi Edie! It was fun to see you after the game. I like you as a friend. Not a girlfriend though. I hope that is okay. From Bob. X

'What's wrong?' Poppy asks, noticing my sad expression as I look down at my phone.

'It's just Bobby. He says he likes me as a friend but doesn't want to be my boyfriend.'

'Don't worry Edie, you'll find someone . . . someone just as brilliant as you!' Poppy says reassuringly. She gives me a big hug.

I look around the room. Georgia goes out with Oscar. Poppy has just started going out with Tom, which makes sense because they always pair up together in rehearsals. Also they lits play husband and wife Cratchit in the play so it makes a lot of sense. Chloe is with Lukas and Pip goes out with a guy from her primary school. They all have boyfriends!

I slump down onto Georgia's bed. 'Thanks, but I really wanted to get a boyfriend before Christmas. It's part of my Boyfriend Plan. Time is running out. I don't want to be the only person in the whole school who doesn't have one!'

'Not *everyone* has a boyfriend, Edie.' Georgia gives me her mug of hot chocolate, because mine is already finished. 'Here. You need this more than me. Anyway, think about all the people in our year. It's absolutely, definitely not everybody, it's only a small percentage. Plus, I'd never had a boyfriend before I went out with Oscar.'

I finish Georgia's hot chocolate and instantly feel better.

'And when you're older, and you're a famous actor, you'll have boys fighting to be your boyfriend!' Pip jokes, making me feel better still.

'What about George McDonald in the year above? He's blind!' Georgia says excitedly.

Pip looks worried.

'Just because Edie is disabled doesn't mean that her boyfriend needs to be disabled too!' Chloe laughs. 'And anyway, I don't think he's blind. He just has a bit of a lazy eye.'

Georgia looks at the floor. I think she's embarrassed; I don't mind though. She's just trying to help out. The more I hang out with Georgia, the more I like her. I'm starting to think it wouldn't be so bad if me, Oscar, and

Georgia formed a trio. We are kind of like the three musketeers!

Pip squeezes my shoulder. 'Anyway, having a boyfriend isn't so great.' She stands up, hands on hips, and announces, 'I'm going to dump Darren next week. I never see him, and when I do, he just talks about his new friends. It's boring.'

Luckily the conversation turns away from my problem to how Pip is going to dump Darren. The logistics sound quite stressful. Maybe they're right. Getting a boyfriend isn't everything.

'I'm just going to put my head on the pillow, but I'm still listening, honest,' Chloe says in the end, as Pip lists all the possible places she could dump Darren: the cinema, bowling alley, shopping centre, the beach, McDonald's . . . But before Pip finishes her sentence, Chloe is out like a light.

Pip and Poppy are next, falling asleep on the double airbed, clearly exhausted from the dumping chat – they both have hot chocolate marks on their faces.

Suddenly, me and Georgia are the

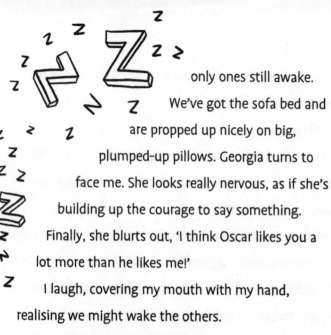

only ones still awake. We've got the sofa bed and are propped up nicely on big, plumped-up pillows. Georgia turns to face me. She looks really nervous, as if she's building up the courage to say something. Finally, she blurts out, 'I think Oscar likes you a lot more than he likes me!'

I laugh, covering my mouth with my hand, realising we might wake the others.

'Absolutely not! We're best friends, but you're his *girlfriend*. He likes you so much. He talks about you all the time!'

Georgia nods slowly, biting her lip. 'No, Edie, he talks about *you* all the time,' she says quietly. 'About how brilliant you are, and the fact you like all of the same things, including all of those Marvel films, and I'm just a bit like, well, why don't you two go out with each other then?'

Gross! 'Because going out with Oscar would be like going out with my brother!' I shiver. 'It would be plain wrong!'

Georgia seems satisfied with my response. 'I've never had a friend who is disabled before. Am I allowed to say that?'

I nod and smile. 'Yes Georgia, "disabled" isn't a swear word, it's just a fact. I am disabled. It's part of me, and without it, I wouldn't be Edie!'

Georgia is starting to look sleepy. She yawns and says, 'Do you ever wish you weren't disabled?'

I think about it. I want to give Georgia a serious answer to her serious question. 'Sometimes, yes. I wish I could tie my shoelaces faster, and I wish I could learn to swim faster, and I even wish I could speak faster, but then I think – well, what's the rush? I get everything done, and I can do everything I want to do, it's just on Edie Time!'

Georgia laughs. 'You might be on Edie Time, but I'm on sleepy time!' She leans across and gives me a big hug. 'Please don't be sad about Bobby, because I think you're brilliant,' she whispers, and falls asleep. And then I do too.

Monday 3.40pm

Mondays are honestly my favourite days now, including the weekend, and it's all because of rehearsals!

In today's rehearsal, we're practising the first half of the play. So far, I have *almost* remembered all of my lines. Nat, who is playing Jacob Marley, keeps getting his lines wrong though.

Mr Murphy keeps raising his eyebrows to the ceiling in despair.

'I wear the chain I forged in life! I made it, erm, erm . . . wait . . .'

'I made it link by link and yard by yard!' I whisper to Nat, when Mr Murphy isn't looking.

Nat winks at me. 'I made it link by link and yard by yard! I gartered it on of my own free will and by my own free will, I wore it!'

'It's a breakthrough for Nathaniel Davis!' Mr Murphy calls, breaking into a most un-Mr-Murphy-like-grin. 'Well done, good sir!'

'Thanks!' Nat whispers to me. 'How do you remember all of your lines *and* my lines?'

I shrug. 'I don't know really. I try and learn the whole play by heart as if it's a song to sing along to on the radio.'

Nat looks dead impressed. 'You don't need any of us. It could be, *A Christmas Carol: A One Woman Play by Edie Eckhart*!' he says.

I laugh. 'No, definitely not. If I had to play all of the parts, at the speed I talk, the play would be eighty-two hours long!'

'Fair enough,' Nat chuckles, and we crack on with the scene.

☆☆☆

After rehearsal, I go to see Flora in her side room. I'm convinced she'll have good advice about who should be my boyfriend, now Bobby is a no-go zone. I could not have been more wrong. When I tell her about the Boyfriend Plan, she looks like she's going to explode. And then she kind of does.

'Why do you want a boyfriend so much anyway?' She stands up. 'It's not everything! I don't have a boyfriend. I thought there was more to you than that. I thought you were better!'

Well this Flora is not the girl I know! I stare at her. One minute, she's really nice, and the next, she's plain harsh.

'Just because you can't get a boyfriend, you shouldn't take it out on me,' I reply, immediately regretting it. Rats, why did I have to say that?

Flora slowly picked up her paintbrushes and left the room. Just like she leaves every conversation recently. I really don't understand her.

‘Stop writing in your book and talk to me, Edie!’ Mum says. I sigh and put down my pen.

I honestly can’t with my mum! First of all she buys me a diary and makes me write more, and then she tells me to stop writing. Make your mind up, woman!

‘How was school, mushroom? How were rehearsals?’ Mum asks, taking my hand in hers. We’re sat in the kitchen, before tea, and I’m really not in a mood to talk to her. I’m afraid that if I talk I am going to burst out crying.

I tell her school was good. ‘Mrs Adler brought her latest baby scan in to show us and her babies look so real!’

‘They are real babies, Edie.’

‘You know what I mean, Ma!’

‘And did you see your new friend Flora at rehearsals?’ That’s a trickier question to answer.

I don’t want to tell her about Flora, and how we argued, because I don’t even know *why* we argued. And if

I did tell Mum, would I have to reveal the Boyfriend Plan?

'Yes, but I didn't talk to her, she looked too busy,' I lie.

Wednesday 6.57pm

Flora didn't show up for rehearsal today. What if it's because of what I said on Monday? I only shouted because she shouted.

I hate arguing. I didn't even mean what I said. Of course Flora could get a boyfriend. He would probably be a really cool skater boy, who was also an artist, and they could talk about brilliant things all the time, and I bet Flora wouldn't run away from him.

At least rehearsal was good today. We talked about costumes and I'm extremely excited about dressing like an old Victorian man. Maybe I should ask Grandad Eric for some of his clothes. I know he's not an old Victorian man, but, you know, same vibe.

I talked to Nat again today. He's completely turned his performance around and has managed to learn ALL his lines since Monday.

I was so impressed.

'I pretended my lines were a song, just like you said!' Nat declared, proudly. He looked at Tom, who raised his eyebrows at him (weird).

160

'So, erm, I was thinking,' said Nat, 'that erm, we could maybe go bowling together on Saturday, on like, a date?'

Okay, where in sausages has that come from? I've never ever even considered Nat to be boyfriend material, and I barely know him. Plus he's not on my original list. But he *does* seem nice, so why not?

How exciting! Yet again, I have got myself a daaaate.

Friday 7.23pm

We're sitting around the kitchen table at Oscar's house, having fish pie. A special Friday after school 'treat' according to the Jenkins family.

'Edie has a date with a boy tomorrow!' Oscar announces, as Elaine pops some peas on our plates.

It's funny, the Jenkins family never ever seem to have secrets from each other. I'd be really humiliated to tell my parents that I was going on a date, but Oscar is never embarrassed to tell his parents anything!

'Oh lovely! Is it another date with Bobby from football?' Elaine asks, giving me a wink.

I shake my head and tell the whole family about Nat from the play. Although I admit I don't know loads about him, I tell them all the stuff about teaching him how to learn lines.

'Learning lines! How romantic!' Elaine gushes. 'I remember my first boyfriend at school.' She sighed fondly. 'Alan Carr.'

'*You* went out with *Alan Carr*?' Charlie giggles.

'Obviously not THE Alan Carr. It was AN Alan Carr.

He's now a dental hygienist in Whitby.'

We all cracked up.

Once we finish laughing, Oscar turns serious. 'Where are you going with Nat?' he asks, looking worried. 'And is he going to look after you?'

'I don't need looking after, Oscar. I can take care of myself!'

Elaine cheers and ruffles Oscar's hair playfully. 'Good on you, Edie! He's always been a fusser, especially when it comes to you. But you know THE story.'

Oscar turns the shade of the ketchup on his plate. He yanks down his hat and crosses his arms. 'Mum! Please don't tell THE story, we've all heard it a million times.'

I love this story. I can't help myself. 'Go on, Elaine, please tell it for the millionth and first time!' I say, knowing that Oscar will hate it.

Elaine begins. 'When Oscar came home from his first day of school, he said, "Mummy, today I met a girl called Edie. She has broke legs and I am going to find a way to make them better!"'

Everybody except Oscar goes 'aww', even Charlie.

Oscar looks fuming. I tap my legs. 'Hurry up mate, they're still not better!' I tease.

'I was such a numpty back then!' Oscar says.

'You were five! We all were!' I say. 'Remember when I thought a wobbly witch had cast a spell on me?'

Elaine laughs and grabs my hand and Oscar's hand. 'Ohhh, you were both so adorable!'

Oscar turns serious again. 'Will you at least let me know where you're going with Nat?' he asks.

I bash his side playfully. 'Erm, Osc, are you my mum? We're just going bowling, chill out! It'll be fun.'

'Okay. Just promise to text me if you need me.'

'I won't!'

'Edie . . .'

'Fine,' I say, rolling my eyes. 'I promise.'

He is such a fusspot sometimes! But at least I know that he cares about me.

Saturday 8.02pm

I'm sitting on the same bench by the sea that I sat on with Flora, but this time I'm alone.

The date with Nat was really bad. Well, it wasn't even a date, it was just horrible. I think about messaging Oscar, but I really want to be independent, and prove that I don't need him all of the time. He can't always be there to protect me from everything.

This is what happened.

I met Nat outside the bowling alley, excited about the evening and wearing my Converse with the brand new bright yellow laces.

When Nat arrived, he didn't say much at all. *That's okay though*, I thought. *I'm nervous too.*

I tried to ask him about his lines again. And when that didn't work, I asked him what his favourite music was. He mumbled something I couldn't hear. Then when we started bowling, he just kept replying to my questions with one word answers and not paying me any attention.

I haven't been on many dates, but I have enough

life experience to know that this one was Bad with a capital B. I mustered all my enthusiasm. 'It's your turn to bowl, Nat!' I said in my most cheerful voice.

Nat looked embarrassed. 'I don't want to be here,' he blurted out, with his head hanging low. 'Tom paid me a tenner to go out with you.'

'Why would he do that?'

Nat shrugged, not meeting my gaze. 'I think he felt sorry for you. I like you, but I don't like you *like that*, if that makes sense.'

'Is it because I'm *different*?' I asked.

Nat stared at his shoes and mumbled, 'Maybe, I don't know.'

My lip wobbled, but I didn't want to cry in front of Nat. Without another word, I walked away and swapped my bowling shoes for my Converse, and now I'm sitting on the bench outside alone. I wish me and Flora hadn't fallen out and she was here now. I wish I could send her a text, but it doesn't feel right.

Why did Flora run away the other night? Does she feel sorry for me too? Mrs Adler was right. Life is harder for

me with my disability. Even though I don't feel different, people look at me like I'm not normal. And certainly not normal enough to get a boyfriend.

Monday 5.30pm

Reading that entry back to myself, two days later, I can see that I was being a little bit dramatic!

I've just finished rehearsal. I avoided talking to Nat and Tom the whole time because it still felt super awks and I didn't want them to know how much they'd really upset me. *Who pays somebody to go out with their friend?*

In other news, I'm currently sitting on the stage, building up the courage to go and find Flora. I miss talking to her.

But before I can, Flora comes over. She sits next to me on the stage, our legs hanging off the front. I think this is the first time I've seen her on stage, and not backstage painting the set.

'I'm sorry I shouted at you last week,' she says. 'I just think you're special enough, without having to get a boyfriend. You don't need one. That's all.'

I smile. 'I'm sorry too,' I say. 'I didn't mean what I said either. You could *easily* get a boyfriend. I reckon you would go out with like a really cool skater boy.'

Flora shakes her head. 'I don't want a cool skater *boy*,' she mutters.

I'm so glad we're friends again. Chatting to Flora is the best part of my week, hands down!

Wednesday 6.49pm

Today's rehearsal was really, really fun.

That's not even an exaggeration. Before Mr Murphy got there, we all placed bets on what 'colour' day he was going to have.

'Orange. A hundred per cent!' Poppy declared. 'Orange tie, orange jumper!'

Just then, Mr Murphy walked in the door, which means he could legit have heard the entire conversation. We all looked at each other and tried not to laugh. The really funny thing was that he was wearing a yellow shirt, yellow tie, and some sort of yellow cravat.

'Now, which of you ragamuffins bet yellow?' Mr Murphy asked, raising an eyebrow. Yikes! He *had* heard us!

I raised my hand, sheepishly.

His face cracked into a grin. 'Eckhart wins! I am glad that my fashion sense amuses you all so much!' Phew! He wasn't angry! That was a super-duper close call!

Mr Murphy watched us perform the second half of the play, and I *nearly* remembered all of my lines without looking at the script. He only needed to prompt me three times (*prompt* is when you forget your lines, so the director reminds you what your line is).

Luckily Nat wasn't at rehearsal, because his character is only in the first bit of the play. Tom was there though, looking a bit shifty. You could cut the tension with a knife.

When it was time for a break, Tom came over. 'I'm sorry I paid Nat to go out with you, Edie. Poppy said you were sad about not having a boyfriend, so I thought it would be a good idea. I thought you might hit it off.'

Poppy hovered behind him like a disappointed mum. 'Obviously it wasn't a good idea, Tom! That's your problem, you think too much. I'm sorry Edie, I had no idea.'

I decided on the spot that I would forgive Tom. There's no point crying over spilt milk, as my dad says. 'Don't worry, both of you. I'm honestly fine now. I've been thinking, maybe I don't actually need a boyfriend!'

Poppy leant in and whispered, 'You and me both. I've

been thinking the same thing!'

'Oi!' Tom laughed. 'I heard that!'

☆☆☆

After the rehearsal I stayed and talked to Flora. She'd brought in the second comic in *The Oracle* series and we sat and read it together. If either Flora or I reached the end of the page before the other one, we'd wait for the other to catch up, before turning the page.

When we got to the end, I had an idea. 'What are you doing on Saturday? Do you want to come to my house for tea?'

Flora nodded and gave a little smile. 'I'd like that.'

☆☆☆

After rehearsal, I found Georgia and Oscar and we walked home together. Georgia hadn't heard the story before, so I filled her in on the horror that was my date with Nat.

'Edie, like I said before, why didn't you ring me? That's why I hate you hanging out with people I don't know!'

'Saying, "I told you so" doesn't make me feel any better, Osc. And you can't protect me from everybody and everything!'

'What about my friend Haz, on the football team, he might go out with you!' Oscar said encouragingly. 'I could ask him?'

I waved my hand at him. I'd forgotten why I wanted a boyfriend in the first place. I think I wanted to fit in with everyone else, but I won't ever fit in, even if I did have a boyfriend. I'd always be 'Edie, the disabled one'. That will always make me different and that's okay. I'm totes fed up of this boyfriend thing. I have bigger fish to fry anyway.

'I'm having another sleepover on Saturday. Do you want to come?' Georgia asked.

'Thanks, I would've loved to, but my friend Flora's coming over to mine for tea!'

Oscar's eyebrow slugs appeared. 'Why didn't you invite me? I'm free!'

We crossed the road. 'Because I want my mum and dad to meet Flora.'

'Well, can I come over and meet Flora?' he asked.

'You sound a bit jealous of Flora, Oscar,' Georgia teased. 'Is Edie only allowed one friend?'

'No, of course not! I just feel like her *best* friend and her new friend should get to know each other,' Oscar explained, trying to sound as relaxed as possible.

I agreed, but now I'm a little bit worried. I like Oscar and Flora so much separately, but I really want them to like *each other*. Oh, holy macaroni, what if they don't get along?

Wednesday 8.54am

Mrs Adler is so pregnant right now. She looks uncomfortable whenever she walks. The other morning you could literally see one of her babies kicking away! She is still just as smiley as ever though.

'Who's your best friend, miss?' I asked Mrs Adler, in tutor today.

She tipped her head to one side, thinking about my question, then shrugged. 'I don't think I have a *best* friend. My wife, maybe, but then I think it's important to have other friendships separate to my marriage. I have friends from school, university, work, and I go to them all for different reasons.'

That made sense. Before starting secondary school, Oscar was my best and only friend. I didn't need any other friends. But now, I have different friends, and I enjoy them for different reasons. I just hope it doesn't mean me and Oscar aren't as close anymore . . .

Saturday 6.12pm

FLORA

I'm really sorry Edie, my mum had a fall today and I don't think I should leave her tonight. Maybe another time x

EDIE

No worries. See you at rehearsal on Monday!

I keep re-reading the text from Flora, and I can't help but feel sooo majorly disappointed. I really wanted my mum and dad to meet her, and I was even getting excited for her and Oscar to hang out.

At least Oscar is on his way round. Maybe we'll play a board game with the fam! *Operation*, that's my dad's favourite. He takes it so seriously.

'Steve, it's a game. You're not at work now!' Mum always moans.

'I need total silence, Angela, this is a serious matter.'

And then when it's my turn, I wobble all over the

176

place and the machine goes wild. Note to self: NEVER become a surgeon!

I hope Oscar gets here soon, I'm getting properly hungry.

> **Flora can't make it, so I guess it's just you and me, baby! More sausage rolls for us ☺ Have you set off yet?**

☆☆☆

Oscar didn't turn up. I can't believe it! Me and Mum watched *Strictly* instead with LOADS of pizza – we had ordered five pizzas for Oscar and Flora to eat with us. Instead of sulking, I ate a whole pizza, and like five sausage rolls, and I even pretended I was one of Mum's friends and kept saying 'oooh, look at him go,' whenever one of the male dancers shook his hips. It was fun, but not as fun as I thought my night would be.

Mum said she understood Flora's reason for cancelling, but she thought Oscar was very rude and that it was hugely out of character. I agree. What is going on?

He was the one who practically begged for an invite. It's so unlike him.

I've just got off FaceTime with Oscar.

He was staring right at the camera with his bobble hat over one of his eyes, almost as if he wanted to hide his face from me. 'I don't see what the big deal is!' he told me. 'I was out with the lads from football and I lost track of time. Flora didn't come either and you didn't shout at her!'

'That's different, Oscar! Flora *told* me she couldn't come. You didn't even text me. You couldn't be bothered! You're supposed to be my best friend.'

'It was clear you didn't want me there anyway,' Oscar muttered. 'You just wanted to spend time with your new best friend Flora.'

179

Oscar's lip wobbled, and he hung up. RUUUUDE!

'Just bog off then!' I shouted at my phone, throwing it down on the bed. I don't think I've ever been this angry.

'All right, Edie?' Dad knocked on my door and joined me on the bed. 'Sorry to be nosy, but I couldn't help overhearing. Is everything okay?'

I shrugged. 'Secondary school is hard.' Wow, just saying those words to Dad felt like a huge relief. 'There's all these rules, and groups, and things to think about, including what Oscar is thinking every minute. I wish I was still Louie's age. All he has to worry about is playing Lego and kicking about in the sand and hanging out with his best friend Ralph.'

'Growing up can be so, so hard.' Dad said, taking my hand. 'I found secondary school difficult too.'

'But wasn't that because you were a mega geek? And you didn't even have the internet or computer games to geek out to! Gosh, you must've been Bored with a capital B!'

He laughed, ruffling my hair. 'It's true, it was a sad life to lead. Anyway, missus! Do you need help learning your lines?'

I nodded, grinning, and handed him my script.

Monday 5.40pm

Mr Murphy is the worst person in the world. He pulled me to one side after rehearsal in the school hall and told me that my acting could be better!

What has got into him? He was singing my praises recently. Now that's all changed.

'You were truly brilliant a week or so ago,' he said. 'But since then you've taken your foot off the gas. You're coasting at about a five out of ten. By opening night, I expect you to be at a ten out of ten.'

Even though Mr Murphy wasn't shouting, it felt like he was telling me off, like I'd done something wrong.

'I know all my lines!' I said, my eyes stinging.

'It's about more than knowing all your lines, Edie,' Mr Murphy said, hand on hip. Today was bright orange day, but clearly even his lurid jumper wasn't cheering him up. 'It's about reading *between* the lines. And sometimes it's about what you don't say. Do you understand what I mean?'

I had no idea what he was going on about. Murphy was speaking in riddles. I nodded and left, because I wanted to get out of there before I burst out crying.

Flora was waiting for me outside – she's started to walk home with me, even though she lives on the other side of town. After she drops me off, she skateboards on to her house. She says she does it because it gives her an excuse to skate more, but secretly I think it's because she likes chatting to me.

I filled Flora in on how horrible Mr Murphy had been. 'I've spent so long perfecting my lines, and still I'm not good enough. I knew I should never have signed up to this.'

Flora frowned, like she always does when she's thinking hard. 'Okay, I'm going to play devil's advocate here.'

I nodded along like I knew what 'devil's advocate' meant. (I've just googled it and it's when you just suggest the other side of the argument, even if you don't believe it.)

'What if Mr Murphy *really* likes you and he knows you're a good actor, and he's only got a grump on to make sure that you're pushing yourself to be the best you can be?'

'That makes absolutely no sense, Flora!'

We had reached my gate. She frowned again. She looked really cute. 'Okay, well, what are you going to do when you get home?'

'I'm going to rehearse Scrooge all night, to prove to stupid ol' Murphy that I am *not* a five out of ten, I am a TEN OUT OF TEN!'

EDIE'S ACTING

Flora nodded, smugly, getting her skateboard ready. 'See Edie! He knows you! He knows that you are stubborn, and brilliant, and that if he gave you a healthy dose of criticism, you would go above and beyond to prove him wrong.'

Damn. Flora was right. Mr Murphy was a sneaky wotsit!

Flora put her foot on her skateboard, then turned back to me. 'I have a football match tomorrow and my mum is coming to watch. Do you want to come? She'd love to meet you.'

I nodded. 'Yes! Sounds great!'

'Amazing, see you tomorrow.' Flora skated forward, kissed my cheek, and then skated down the street and disappeared around the corner.

Tuesday 3.30pm

I'm sitting with Flora's mum, Sara, at the football match, eating lemon drizzle cake and drinking hot chocolate. Football has never been so fun!

Sara's an electric wheelchair user, which was a proper pain for her to drive on the muddy grass, but we got here in the end. Well, I say 'we', but I didn't do anything. Flora pushed Sara and I carried the flask of hot chocolate. I noticed Oscar warming up for a game on the opposite field and waved at him, but I think he pretended not to notice me.

Flora is a really great footballer and she makes me forget how much I don't rate football. 'YES!' I jump up and down at both of her goals.

During the first half, after the excitement of the goal scoring, me and Sara chat about Flora. Sara seems very different to Flora. She's chatty, like me.

'My darling daughter is a worrier, and takes everything far too seriously,' Sara laughs. 'Sometimes I think she's the grown-up and I'm the child!'

I tell her that I agree. Flora *does* take everything a bit seriously, but it makes her unique. Sara smiles when I say that. 'Thank you for looking after my Flora. She doesn't stop talking about you at home!'

Sara's words make my tummy jump. *Weird!* Then the referee blows her whistle for half time and Flora runs over to us.

'Oi! This cake isn't for you, I made it for me and Edie!' Sara teases, when Flora, muddy and sweaty, grabs a giant slice.

In between all the fun I'm having, I can't help thinking about Osc. Every so often, I look over at his pitch, but it's too far away to see what he's up to. Everyone just looks like little dots. It's only been a couple of days, but Oscar and I have never gone this long without talking. I miss him and I just wish I could have my best friend back. I wish he'd cheesing apologise for not coming over though.

But for now I am going to focus on the positives. I'm here watching Flora play football (which I somehow don't hate) with Flora's really nice mum – life is pretty good!

'I've loved being your tutor this term, and I'm so sad to be leaving you. But I'll be back for when you start Year 8, which won't be long now!'

It's Mrs Adler's last day of school before she goes on maternity leave, and I already miss her, even though she's standing right in front of me! I think back to September, when I thought she was the worst person in the world. I could not have been more wrong.

Recently, I've been thinking that Oscar and I probably did depend on each other a bit too much. And that it's okay for us to have other friends. I think Mrs Adler was the first person to make me realise that. Looking back, I think she saw something in me that I didn't see in myself.

After tutor group, I stay behind and give Mrs Adler a present for her babies.

Mrs Adler tears off the wrapping paper and laughs out loud. 'Bert and Ernie cuddly toys for my Bert and Ernie. Thank you so much, Edie!' she says, giving me a big hug, and wiping her eyes. 'Oh I'll miss you! Break a leg in the school play. I know you'll be amazing. I just knew you'd make a brilliant actor!'

Why did everybody know I'd enjoy acting before I did? Do I even know myself? This is unbelievable.

This weekend is my favourite weekend of the year, because it is the run-up to Christmas when me and my mum go shopping for presents. We walk around town all day until our legs ache, and then we go to the Christmas market by the harbour and have hot chocolate and mince pies. DREAM. DAY.

My Christmas present list was really easy this year. I've used one of the blank pages at the back of my diary to write my list:

MUM: Big fancy candle
DAD: Camping torch
LOUIE: Lego
OSCAR:
FLORA: Sketchbook and pencils

I feel confident in my gift choices this year and I hope everybody will like them. It's always really tricky for me to buy Mum's present without her knowing what it is, but there's normally a point in the day when she disappears to do secret stuff for my birthday (which is next week! YAY!).

I keep staring at the gap after Oscar's name. For the first time ever I have no idea what to get him. Usually getting Oscar's gift is the easiest thing in the world, because I get something he's been talking about, or something that I know he'll really like. But I haven't properly spoken to him in ages, so I have lits no idea what to get him.

I'm going to see him tomorrow; we made a plan for him to come over. We haven't spoken since our big argument, so fingers crossed he apologises to me and we can be friends again. And hopefully I'll work out what present to get him for Christmas. If not, I'll message Georgia.

Before going shopping, though, it's time to read through my lines. It's getting close to crunch time and I really want Mr Murphy to change his tune about my performance. On the night, I will be the bee's knees, and the cat's pyjamas (i.e. good).

Sunday 3.10pm

This is torture.

Me and Oscar are both sat in my bedroom and we could not be further away from each other. He's sitting on a beanbag, playing a game on his phone, and I am writing on my bed.

'You're always writing nowadays. I thought you hated the idea of keeping a diary,' he says, glancing up from his phone.

It's the first thing he's said to me all day, so, yay, progress?

I shrug. 'I think it's grown on me. I enjoy it.'

'You like that thing more than you like me.' He laughs, but I can tell that he isn't joking. He goes back to playing on his phone.

I glare at him. 'Oscar, you're being ridiculous!'

'Okay, let me write in it then.' He comes to sit on the bed next to me.

O: I like this book more than I like Oscar.

E: Not true. Oscar is my best friend.

O: But since starting secondary school I have made new friends at drama rehearsal and I don't need Oscar anymore.

I can't believe my eyes. Oscar thinks I don't *need* him anymore? Where did that come from? *He* was the one who made new friends first and got a new hobby. Why can't he be happy for me?

I am speechless. I pick up my pen again. I can't even look at him. I can hear him kicking the carpet in a huff.

Eventually he speaks, and his voice is cracking and croaky, as if he's trying to stop himself from crying.

Oscar tells me that he's jealous of my drama rehearsals, and since I started the play, he has barely seen me. This makes me so angry. Oscar was the one to join the football team and get other friends, Oscar was the one to get a girlfriend and spend all day, every day, snogging her face off, and Oscar was the one who was too busy to hang out. So why am I the one to blame? This is not fair, at all.

'Why is it one rule for you and another for me?' I say. 'You're always at football practice, so why can't I do after school drama club?'

Oscar shrugs. 'And when you fell over last week, you didn't even need my help!'

So he was angry at me for not needing him as much? Having somebody relying on you for practical things is totally not the same as friendship.

'You don't want to be my friend, you want to be my carer!' I snap.

Even though they are only words, Oscar looks as if I've physically slapped him. His eyes fill up with tears and he storms out of my room. Then I hear the front door slam.

I lie on my bed, determined not to cry. I flick to my Christmas present list:

MUM: Big fancy candle ✓
DAD: Camping torch ✓
LOUIE: Lego ✓
OSCAR:
FLORA: Sketchbook and pencils ✓✓

Monday 1.12pm

I've decided I'm not apologising to Oscar until he apologises to me.

I'm going to try and forget about the stupid argument, and enjoy my day. I've already had some brilliant news. This morning our supply teacher told us that Mrs Adler has given birth to two baby girls!

Apparently they were born last night. One at ten minutes *to* midnight, and the other one at five *past* midnight, so although they are twins, they have different birthdays. How funny is that?

The babies are called Anya and Lily. I'm not going to lie, I am a bit disappointed that Mrs Adler and her wife didn't actually go for Bert and Ernie but I won't tell her that!

☆☆☆

Yes! This has been a great day! And on top of it all, WE FINALLY HAD PIZZA IN REHEARSAL!

Today, we rehearsed the play right from the beginning

to the end and, although there were a *lot* of mistakes from us all, we got there!

'That . . . was not a complete disaster!' Mr Murphy said at the end, which, coming from him, was like the biggest compliment of all time.

After, as a reward, we got pizza. We all sat in a big circle, like we did at the beginning of rehearsals all those months ago, only this time we didn't have to say interesting facts about ourselves because we all know each other so well. I ended up sitting next to Nat, which wasn't ideal.

'I'm really sorry, Edie,' he said quietly. 'I shouldn't have agreed to go on the date and I shouldn't have been rude to you during the date. I should've just been honest with you. I still really like you as a friend.'

I shook my head. 'There's no need to apologise. I should thank you. At least I've got the worst date of my life out the way, fingers crossed at least. And I'm only eleven!'

He laughed. And then to my surprise Flora joined the circle, taking the seat on the other side of me and propping her skateboard up next to her chair. It was great! Tom and Poppy leant across and we talked about the play.

'Are you nervous Edie, about opening night?' Poppy asked.

'Honestly, I haven't really thought about it yet.' I've been too busy learning lines, buying Christmas presents and arguing with Oscar, who I haven't talked to all week.

'Flora, that skateboard is amazing!' Tom said. And then they were off, chatting away about skating, while me, Poppy and Nat chatted more about the play and gave each other some last-minute tips about how to calm our nerves before opening night. We all discovered that we have bath bombs we haven't used yet, so we're going to crack those open over the next week, and have baths of dreams. That sounds legit like something you'd do to chill out those play jitters.

'Okay gang, pick up your crusts and get on home. See you all next Monday, when our own Scrooge will be one year older!' Mr Murphy said, smiling and nodding towards me.

Poppy clapped her hands. 'It's your birthday, Edie! When?'

I told her it's on Sunday, and she's decided to organise a party. At least it will be a distraction from the fact that it's obvious I won't be spending it with Oscar like usual doing the three M's. I miss the three M's!

☆☆☆

On the way home, I filled Flora in about the argument I had with Oscar. Flora looked thoughtful, but then changed the subject to my birthday. I told her that I don't want a big fuss.

Flora laughed. 'Bad luck. Poppy's already set up an 'Edie's secret birthday party' WhatsApp group and her plans sound pretty . . . *elaborate*!'

We'd reached the park near my house. 'Show me the messages,' I said.

'No way.'

I tried to take Flora's phone out of her hand, but she pulled it away.

'Oi! It's a big surprise!'

I wouldn't be defeated. I lunged at Flora and grabbed for her phone, but she was too fast for me. As I swooped,

I lost my balance, and fell. She tried to grab me and I landed on top of her. It was Hilarious with a capital H. We both laughed so much my tummy started hurting.

Eventually we stopped laughing, but we stayed lying side by side on the grass. 'Do you want to come to my house on Saturday, for a pre-birthday dinner?' Flora asked.

'Sounds great!' And then we lay there for ages, not talking, just looking up at the clouds in the sky.

'I mean, talk about clichés Mum' Flora said. 'The first time Edie comes to our flat, we have ramen. We should've worn kimonos – you know, just to really make it clear that we're Japanese!'

All three of us laughed. I was glad Sara made noodle soup. Even though it's hard for me to eat, it's really, really tasty, and one of my favourite meals.

Flora's mum flexed her wrists and her fingers, as if in pain. 'Flora love, will you cut up my noodles? My hands are starting to ache.'

Whilst still munching on her noodles, Flora took her mum's bowl and cut up the noodles into easy mouthfuls for her.

Without asking, Flora smiled and took my bowl to cut up my noodles. I hope she doesn't think I'm a nuisance.

'What film are you going to watch after tea?' Sara asked.

At the same time as I said '*Thor,*' Flora said '*Wonder Woman.*'

We looked at each other with cross expressions, but

almost immediately burst out laughing.

'Fine,' Flora sighed, grinning. 'I guess it's the birthday girl's choice, *Thor* it is!'

'Actually,' I said, 'I've seen *Thor* like, a million times. Let's watch *Wonder Woman*!'

☆☆☆

I didn't want to admit to Flora how much I loved *Wonder Woman*, but it was so cool. DC isn't *completely* awful after all! But I would never tell Flora that. I'm still sure that Marvel is better. Deep down, she must know that too.

We shared a blanket to keep warm, and put salt and sweet popcorn in a bowl, and Sara tipped a packet of Minstrels in.

When the film ended, Flora looked nervous. 'I know it's not officially your birthday yet, but technically it's only three hours away, and I know there'll be loads of people there tomorrow, so I thought that I could give you your present now?'

I nodded eagerly, and she reached down and pulled

out a small package, wrapped up with brown paper and string.

I untied the string bow and carefully unwrapped the present. I couldn't believe my eyes.

'I know it's silly . . .' she said.

'I love it!' I managed to say this time. It was beautiful.

I kissed her on the cheek and hugged her for a long time. When we let go, I saw that Flora was a bit red. I felt my cheeks go red too, like her going red made me go red.

It was the best present I'd ever got in my whole life. Hands down.

Sunday 10.05pm

I am officially twelve – woo hoo!

I've had a lovely day. I've been spoilt, like *so much*. My mum and dad got me an *insanely* cool three-wheeled bike. It's even got a seat at the back that Louie can sit on. We went for a ride to the seaside this morning and Louie squealed for the whole journey, I think he was having an even better time than me!

And then Poppy picked me up for my birthday party surprise. We went to Laser Quest!

I swear Poppy is an old lady in an eleven-year-old's body. Before booking Laser Quest, she'd rung up to double-check that somebody with cerebral palsy could play the game safely. She'd also double-checked with my mum that she was happy for me to play Laser Quest. She's very sweet.

'If anything, Edie, it's *safer* than real life,' Poppy said, on the way in the car. 'Essentially it's just one massive bouncy castle. If you fall over, you won't hurt yourself!'

When we got to Laser Quest, everyone was there: Tom, Nat, Chloe, Georgia, Lukas, Pip, and Flora. Just no

Oscar. It did feel strange, but I didn't want to bring the mood down.

Georgia beamed when she saw me. 'I tried to make Oscar come too,' she said. 'But I feel like he's been avoiding me recently, it's weird.'

That IS weird. It's one thing for Oscar not to be talking to me, but Georgia as well? I don't want him to be lonely.

'Now let's go shoot everybody!' Nat screamed, a little too enthusiastically. It sounded quite sinister actually. And we entered the game.

It was loads of fun. Near the end of our game, I fell over, but like Poppy had said, because the floor was inflatable, it didn't hurt at all. Even though I couldn't make it to my feet, I made the most of the situation. I crawled into a corner, where I was out of sight, and I became a sneaky sniper! Every time somebody ran around the corner, I'd shoot them before they saw me.

'Hey, Edie, that's cheating!' Poppy moaned, after I'd laser shot her straight in the chest. She sprinted off around the corner.

'No it's not,' I shouted after her. 'It's being smart . . .

and not being able to get up!'

I was getting ready to shoot the next person coming round the corner, when I saw it was Flora. 'Psst! Flora! Over here!'

Flora laughed and crawled over to join me. 'Edie, are you there on purpose, or are you stuck?'

'Erm. Maybe a bit of both?'

Flora grinned and squeezed my hand, leaving hers on top of my hand for a moment. For the rest of the session we became a team, hiding and shooting everybody who ran around the corner unsuspectingly. WE WON!

It turns out that a load of shooting makes everyone starving hungry, so after the game was over, my parents and Poppy's mum arrived and took us all to the diner where they served *massive* pizzas. I sat in between Georgia and Flora.

'I'm so hungry,' I exclaimed. 'I bet I could finish a whole pizza to myself!'

They really were huge pizzas. To put it into context,

my mum, dad, Louie and Poppy's mum were sharing one between the four of them.

Everybody laughed. 'Well, you *are* the birthday girl!' Poppy's mum said. 'If you want a whole pizza to yourself, then that's what you should have!'

I'm not even exaggerating, when the pizza came it was legit three times the size of my head.

'Edie, mate, you can't finish that! You'll explode!' Nat said, looking worried for me.

I did it though! And as I ate my last crust, the whole table cheered and clapped. I grinned, my face covered with tomato sauce and a rogue piece of ham. Mum and Dad looked very proud of me.

'I never doubted you. Well done, birthday girl!' Flora beamed, handing me a napkin.

At bedtime, and post bath-bomb bath of dreams, I

snuggled up, very full and happy and probably legit covered in glitter and smelling of vanilla. I was about to read my *Speedy Edie* comic for like the millionth time. And then I got a text.

FLORA

I've loved spending this weekend with you.
Happy Birthday. Lots of love x

I think I fell asleep smiling.

Monday 6.50pm

My first official day in my duodenary year (duodenary just means 'twelfth' – I learnt it from Mr Murphy today!) and it's not been a bad one!

Mr Murphy brought chocolate birthday cake to the rehearsal. A couple of the cast grumbled about me being Mr Murphy's favourite (I probs am), but their moaning stopped as soon as they realised that they'd get a slice of cake out of it.

Flora stopped painting for ten minutes to enjoy some cake with us.

'Sir, Edie and Flora cheated at Laser Quest yesterday!' Poppy teased.

'We didn't cheat, we were clever and stealthy!' Flora said, winking at me. *She's definitely coming out of her shell a bit!*

After rehearsal, I texted Mum, asking whether I could stay behind for half an hour longer to help Flora finish the set. She's nearly done.

MUM

Of course love, I'll pick you up in a bit.

Give Flora my love xxx

'My mum says hello,' I told Flora. 'She properly loves you!'

'And my mum loves you too! She won't stop banging on about you.'

We laughed, and I thought back to how lovely Saturday night was when I went over to Flora's. Then something crossed my mind. Better out than in, I reckon.

I took a deep breath. 'I don't want you to feel like you have to look after me, like you look after your mum. You don't need to cut up my noodles for me. I never want to feel like I'm a burden.'

Flora shook her head. 'I don't feel like I *have* to do anything, I do it because I want to. I do it because I *care* about you.'

My stomach flipped.

'And I'm not the only person who cares about you, Edie,' Flora continued. 'Oscar cares about you too. There's a big difference between caring, and being a carer.

Sometimes you're really stubborn, Edie Eckhart. There's nothing wrong with people helping you every now and then, if it makes life easier. But also, you know your own capabilities, which is why I'd never help when it wasn't needed. Do you see what I'm saying?'

I nodded. Flora is very wise! And now I know I have to patch things up with Oscar.

Tuesday 5.25pm

I'm waiting at the side of the field for Oscar to finish his football match. Why am I so nervous? All I'm doing is waiting to speak to my best friend in the whole wide world, that's it. Over the years, I must've talked to Oscar thousands of times, probably hundreds of thousands of times – I mean, who's counting anyway?

I'm shaking, and it's nothing to do with my cerebral palsy, or how cold it is (and actually it is pretty chilly). I wrap my scarf tighter around my neck. I know it's because deep down I'm afraid that me and Oscar will argue again.

The bottom line is, I *want* Oscar to see the play. I want him to see what I've been working on this term. But, more than that, I want him to see that I haven't replaced him; I've just found this brilliant new side of me. I hope he can see how happy acting makes me.

Oh fiddlesticks and fish, he's walking up to me now. My tummy is doing somersaults.

I wave. 'Hey Oscar, good match?' I ask, scuffing the grass with my Converse, trying to act casual and cheerful.

Oscar shrugs and pulls his bobble hat further down his head, which isn't a good sign, let's be honest. 'It was all right.'

'Cool, well I thought you might want to come to the Christmas play on Thursday. Georgia's coming, so maybe you could sit with her?'

Oscar mumbles something indecipherable and takes the ticket. He doesn't even look at me. And then he turns and walks away.

I can't believe my ears or my eyes. Oscar is lits being SO rude right now.

I take a deep breath and close my eyes; something Mr Murphy tells us we have to do before saying our biggest lines.

'I didn't mean what I said,' I shout after him. 'Of *course* I know you're not my carer. I just sometimes rely on you too much. You're still my best friend.'

Oscar turns around, a small smile forming, but not quite big enough for me to feel like everything is okay. 'You're still my best friend too, Edie,' he says sadly. 'Thanks for the ticket.'

I felt super nervous at rehearsal today, and I kept forgetting all of my lines.

'I'm so sorry, Mr Murphy,' I say. 'I know my lines, honestly!'

'I know you do, Edie,' he says gently. 'Remember, take deep breaths, you've got this.'

How does he know I've got this?

I've lits never done anything like this in my whole, entire life and suddenly it's all feeling a bit too real. What if I'm not good enough and everybody laughs at me because I'm a genuinely awful actor.

What if I spend the rest of my school years being laughed at and mocked?

'Oh here she comes, Edie Eckhart. Remember when she tried to play Scrooge and she forgot all her lines, fell over in front of everybody AND her pants fell down?'

I take deep breaths, and try to do what Mr Murphy says.

It will be okay, won't it?

After rehearsal, Flora and I walk home together. I hope it won't be the last time, but I can't help worrying that life will go back to normal after the play. What if Flora only likes me as Scrooge?

We head in the direction of our bench, even though it's a bit out of the way of the usual route home. We haven't said it's 'our bench', but we both know it is; at least, I hope Flora feels the same. We sit down next to each other side by side, looking out at the bluey–grey sea and the chattering seagulls overhead.

'Take in the sea air,' Flora says. 'It'll do you good. It'll make you feel better and calm those wavy nerves of yours.'

I take a big breath up my nose but all I can smell is stinky seaweed and greasy old chips.

'Do you mind if I write a bit?' I say. 'It calms me down.'

'Of course not,' Flora says, smiling.

I open my diary, but continue chatting to Flora. 'I hope tomorrow goes well. I feel the pressure of everybody relying on me and I don't want to let them all down. By this time tomorrow, the play will be done, and the end of term will be here. I can't believe I've nearly done a whole term at secondary school already; it's flown by.'

Flora laughs. 'Edie, I thought you said you wanted to write and calm down. You're talking a mile a minute! Is it making you feel better?'

'Much, much better.' I stand, ready to walk home, feeling on cloud nine.

Thursday 10.45pm

I've only got a few more pages left in this diary! I've asked Mum for a brand-spanking new diary for Christmas and she's very happy about it. But at this point I'm not sure I'll make it to Christmas.

Christmas is on the other side of this performance and right now I don't know if I'll be able to get through it.

I'm in the wings, waiting for my cue to go on stage. My butterflies are out of control, spinning, flipping – you name it, they are doing it. I'm dressed in Grandad Eric's trousers, braces and flat-cap, and I feel a bit stupid to be honest. The trousers look massive on me!

I know Mr Murphy will be in the front row with a copy of the script, ready to prompt us if we need him to. But even so, just knowing all of those people will be looking at me playing Scrooge . . . What if I Scrooge it up? Oh no, oh no, oh no.

'Are you okay, Edie?' Poppy asks me, squeezing my arm. 'You're as pale as one of the ghosts!'

'Pops, what if everybody thinks I'm rubbish? I *feel* rubbish, and I look ridiculous!'

Poppy looks down at my clown-like pants. 'You do look a *bit* ridiculous to be honest!'

Why doesn't this feel quite right? I want to play Scrooge, but I don't feel like Scrooge. I feel like a big, silly man, in a big, silly costume.

Unless I'm *not* a big silly man. LIGHTBULB MOMENT!

'Poppy, how long have we got until the play starts?'

'Erm, seven minutes. Why?'

'I have an idea, and I need your help!'

☆☆☆

I wish I'd had a camera to capture Mr Murphy's face when I walked out on stage in a skirt and a big Victorian hat. He smiled, but his face couldn't hide how he was feeling. He was *nervous* . . . and majorly confused.

That's why it didn't feel quite right before. Because I was dressed like a man. And I didn't want to play a man. I wanted to play somebody I could relate to. I thought back to my notes, before my audition:

Why can't Scrooge be female?

It didn't take much to 'female up' Scrooge. I borrowed one of Poppy's spare skirts and I asked her to give the gang the nod to say 'her' instead of 'his', 'she' instead of 'he' and 'Ms Scrooge' instead of 'Mr Scrooge'. Simple with a capital S!

By making Scrooge a woman, I was making a point that girls are just as capable as boys. *And* girls can be just as moody as boys (just ask Flora, ha ha!).

I loved seeing everybody else perform. They absolutely smashed their roles. Nat remembered all of his lines, giving me a cheeky wink at the end of his scene, and Poppy was peak Mrs Cratchit, bossing everybody about. You could see that Tom, who played her husband, was genuinely terrified of her!

Halfway through the play, just as Ms Scrooge had met the Ghost of Christmas Past and was about to meet the Ghost of Christmas Present, I looked out at the audience. There were so many people looking at me.

I saw Mum, Dad, Louie and Grandad Eric, all in the second row, looking so happy and proud.

Rats on toast. What was my next line? My mind had gone totes blank.

I took two deep breaths and walked to my point on the stage, next to a piece of scenery, a brilliant old Victorian house. *Flora painted this,* I thought, smiling to myself. But as I looked closer at the painted board, I saw a little note. Written in teeny, tiny writing, it said,

'Edie, don't worry, you've got this!'

My heart felt so full. *She's only gone and left me a note!*

Suddenly, my brain filled with all my lines, as if a dam had been opened. The words began to rush out of my mouth.

The rest of the play sped by, and I did not stop. The audience laughed at the funny bits, and I could see my mum crying at the sad bits. I couldn't remember a time when I had felt happier. I was a proper actor!

At the end of the play, we all held hands and bowed. Poppy squeezed my hand, and when we went backstage she gave me the biggest hug ever. 'You were amazeballs, Ms Scrooge!' she squealed.

Mr Murphy cleared his throat behind us. 'So Eckhart changes the gender of the main character at the last second and she doesn't think about telling the creative director, eh?'

I went bright red. 'Sir, I just thought I—'

He put his hand up and I shut up immediately. OMG I am gonna get told off BIG TIME.

'I thought you were marvellous,' he said, and his face broke out into the biggest grin I've ever seen.

PHEW!

Mum ran at me after the performance. 'Come here, love, our very own actor!' she screeched, giving me the biggest hug ever, which was a real achievement for my mum who is the queen of big hugs.

'All right, my turn, I didn't know my daughter was a bona fide grumpy old woman.' Dad winked. 'I hope you didn't take inspiration from me!'

I laughed and shook my head, giving my dad an equally big hug. Then I looked towards Grandad Eric. 'Was I better than Judi Dench, Grandad?'

'Judi who?' he joked. He grabbed me and hugged me tight. 'Did I spot a bit of me in that there Mrs Scrooge?' I laughed and nodded. Totally busted.

Next up was Louie who ran at me, hugging my legs tightly.

'I liked it when the ghost chased you, Didi!' Louie said. 'It was funny!'

'Thanks, Lou!' I said, ruffling his hair.

Someone tapped me on the shoulder. *Oscar!* I hadn't seen him in the audience. He must have been at the back.

'Can we chat? Outside maybe?' he asked. I'm not sure I'd ever seen him look that awkward in my entire life.

Mum and Dad nodded, still beaming and glowing from my performance. Mr Murphy was now talking to them about what a natural actor I was.

On the way out of the hall, people kept stopping me to say, 'Well done, Edie'. Even people I didn't know! If this is what a celebrity lifestyle is like, sign me up! Red carpet, here I come!

'Best Scrooge I've ever seen!'

'Scrooge is much better as a woman! You were awesome!'

Eventually, after I had practically elbowed my way out of the school hall, utterly crowded by my adoring fans, Oscar and I found a quiet spot on the school field. It was freezing.

'Edie, you were brilliant tonight,' he said. 'So great. I couldn't believe it! I've always known you can act, but that was another level.'

I prodded him jokily in his ribs. 'Oi! There's no need to sound so surprised!'

Oscar laughed. 'I'm not, I always knew you were brilliant, but I didn't know you were *that* brilliant!'

I couldn't help but smile. 'Thanks Oscar. I've missed you.'

Maybe it was wrong to be so honest with him, but the truth was, I *had* missed him. It was like the penny had just dropped. No matter how many friends I had, Oscar would always be my best friend. It's just the way it is.

'I've missed you too. Which is why . . . I will,' Oscar said firmly. He shut his eyes tightly and leant towards me.

I was so lost. What was Oscar chatting on about? 'You will . . . what?'

Oscar opened one eye and flung his arms wide, wobbling ever so slightly. 'I will go out with you,' he declared. 'I will be your boyfriend.'

Oscar wanted to be my boyfriend? This made no sense. Or was it the opposite? Did it make complete sense?

'What about your GIRLFRIEND Georgia?' I asked.
'I broke up with her. Because I missed you. And Charlie said it was the most obvious solution!' *Oh, no,* I thought. *Poor Georgia!*

I sat down on the damp grass and I took a few moments to consider what he was saying.

'Soo . . .' Oscar rocked back and forth on his feet. 'Does this mean we're going out now?'

'Please help me up!' I reached up for Oscar's hand. 'I didn't realise the grass was going to be THIS wet!'

Oscar pulled me up and laughed at my damp Victorian skirt. 'You look like you've wet yourself!' he snorted.

And suddenly it was the most hilarious thing. We laughed so much, I almost weed myself. After, I held his hand. 'I love you, Oscar.'

We swung our hands back and forth. 'I love you too, Edie,' he said. 'Which is why it just makes sense if we—'

'NO!' I shouted, so loudly that Oscar yelped and jumped. 'Shut your eyes.'

Oscar looked confused. He reluctantly closed his eyes, still holding my hand.

'Imagine kissing Georgia.' I watched. Oscar couldn't help it. He grinned, widely.

'Now, imagine kissing me.' He frowned, trying his best to fake a smile.

'Now open your eyes. You don't want to kiss me,' I said matter-of-factly. 'And I do *not* want to kiss you! Just because we make great best friends, doesn't mean we should be boyfriend and girlfriend.'

'But I thought you wanted a boyfriend.'

'Yeah, Oscar, I thought I did. But actually I don't want just anyone. I want someone who gives me butterflies, someone I actually *want* to kiss and hopefully somebody who actually *wants* to kiss me!'

He nodded, looking extremely relieved.

'Basically, don't ever take advice from Charlie. What does she know?'

Oscar laughed. 'You'll find someone perfect for you eventually, I know it. Somebody who makes you feel like the most special person in the world.'

My stomach flipped. *Holy macaroni!* I looked back towards the school.

Just then, my parents and Grandad Eric walked over.

Dad was carrying Louie on his back. 'Are you okay, love? Are you two friends again?'

'Yeah,' Oscar said, looking at me. 'So, are we best friends again or what?'

'Of course! Marvel marathon at mine tomorrow?'

'Sounds brilliant!' Oscar spotted Georgia and ran at a full speed pelt towards her. *You go, Glen Coco.*

Mum and Dad beamed. 'We'll get fish and chips in for tea, love,' Mum said.

'Great! Please can I just go and say goodbye to someone first?'

Louie had fallen asleep from all the excitement. 'Of course you can! We'll pop Louie in the car, no rush, you superstar!'

'Thanks, Dad.'

The hall was empty by the time I got back, apart from one person. And it was just the person I wanted to see.

Flora and I sat down, our legs dangling over the stage.

We sat in silence for a bit and I reflected on secondary school so far. I feel like a completely different person. When I think about who Edie Eckhart was at the start of this year, when I began this diary, I barely recognise her.

Now, I feel so much happier. School's great, I've found acting, and my new friends are brilliant.

It's funny, it's the end of term and I've just realised . . . I failed my task. I don't have a boyfriend. I seem to have got distracted by the play, and new friends, and Flora.

'Did Oscar ask you out just now?' Flora said quietly.

I nodded, and I noticed her shoulders slump down.

'I said no,' I told her. 'I mean, he's my best friend and that's how it will always be.' I paused. My heart felt like it was in my throat. 'Also he doesn't give me butterflies . . . like you do.'

I said out loud what I'd just realised today. The hand-holding, the stomach jolts, the times we'd laughed, talked, didn't talk, the times on our bench, and the times we just lay on the grass in silence. I liked Flora! More and more each time I hung out with her.

I didn't want a boyfriend; I wanted a *girlfriend*. Flora.

But instead of responding, Flora jumped off the stage and walked away, not looking back.

Edie, you plonker! I thought. Why did you have to go and say that, you big buffoon?

I watched as Flora walked to the far corner of the room and picked up a bunch of flowers, a prop from the play.

Oh thank holy chicken nuggets. She was coming back!

Flora climbed up the stage steps and handed the flowers to me. 'I want to tell you that you're brilliant, and funny, and the best person I have ever met. You are AMAZING, Edie Eckhart!'

Flora closed her eyes and held my hands. OMG. It was *actually* happening. I was about to KISS Flora. This was unreal! I shut my eyes and . . . OUCH. My teeth hit Flora's train-tracks. It. Hurt.

We both burst out laughing. After a minute, I said, 'You're still wrong about DC by the way, Marvel is the best! Apart from *The Oracle*. That's the one exception.'

Flora laughed and rolled her eyes.

'Do you want to come round for tea tomorrow?' I

said. 'You can *finally* meet Oscar!'

Flora smiled, and for the millionth time that term I got butterflies in my tummy, because of her. 'Sounds great.'

And then we walked out of the school hall together, holding hands.

Acknowledgements

I don't know where to even begin! This is harder than writing the book.

Thank you to my editor Polly Lyall-Grant and my copy-editor Genevieve Herr for taking my rambles about sausage rolls and seagulls, and making them make much more sense. And to everybody at Hachette Children's for making my twenty-five-year-old dream of becoming a children's author into a reality.

To Flo, Lily, Katy and everybody else in the Off The Kerb family. You make me feel like a superstar each and every day, and without your constant support, I'd be a mess. Thank you for reminding me to eat and sleep regularly. Goooooooo team!

To my friends and family, all of them, and too many to mention. The Huddersfield lot, the telly gang, my comedy comrades and everybody else in between. Thank you for being patient, caring, and understanding when it takes me three weeks to reply to your texts!

To Rowena, who should be here to knock me down a peg or two, making sure I keep my feet firmly placed on the ground even though I'm a big-deal author. I miss you, Ro.

To Richard Hirst, my English teacher. You saw the writer in me long before I saw it in myself. But please, please don't mark this book; I still live in fear of your red pen.

Thank you to Ollie, my very own Louie. You might be a foot taller than me, and moustached-up, but you'll always be my baby brother, and my best friend. I love you loads.

And last but certainly not least, thank you to Andrea and Rob, my Mum and Dad. I am who I am today because of your unwavering faith in my abilities. You were the most brilliant lockdown buddies whilst I wrote this book, keeping me topped up on tea, cake and words of encouragement.

ROSIE JONES Is a comedian, actor and scriptwriter, who has cerebral palsy. Rosie is a regular on popular comedy shows including *The Last Leg, Mock the Week, 8 Out of 10 Cats Does Countdown* and *Hypothetical*.

Rosie has written for *Sex Education* and hosts the podcast *Daddy Look at Me* with Helen Bauer. Rosie is incredibly excited to be a children's author – Jacqueline Wilson is her personal hero!